KU-452-931

The Swordsmen

PRAISE FOR OTHER NOVELS
by DICK WYBROW

Hell inc.

Wow! What a book! I laughed constantly. On top of it being funny it's well written to boot.
-- Scott Luttrell, Amazon Reviewer

I read at night, before I fall asleep. My husband has yelled at me several times for laughing out loud and waking him up. -- Kope, GoodReads reviewer

Not since reading Hitchhiker's Guide the first time have I so laughed out loud. This book was can't-put-down good. -- Bobbi Shockley, Amazon Reviewer

The Mentor

"This truly is a masterpiece." -- Corey Foley

"No question, The Mentor is a powerful thriller -- but it's also funny."
-- Brad Meltzer, New York Times bestselling author

Copyright © Dick Wybrow 2019

www.dickwybrow.com

Edited by A.M. Miller

This is a work of fiction. Names, characters, places and incidents either are the product of the author's imagination or are used fictitiously. Any resemble to actual persons, living or dead, is entirely coincidental.

All rights reserved

Without limiting the rights under copyright reserved above, no part of this publication may be reproduced, stored in or introduced into a retrieval system, or transmitted, in any form or by any means (electronic, mechanical, photocopying, recording or otherwise), without the prior written permission of the copyright owner of this book.

Preface

9 January, 2019
Auckland, New Zealand

I began writing this book you're holding… one night in Atlanta, Georgia on a dare.

That evening, in a low-boil rage of red-wine-fueled jealousy, I was kvetching about the runaway success of a novel about a young girl who meets a rich guy who spanks her with a leather belt.

Wait. Before I go any further, I would like to say that like anyone who works hard, EL James deserves her success. The dream happened; it became a hit. So what if it wasn't Shakespeare? People liked it. But, man, many *more* people like shredding the books, especially those who'd likely never read them. I didn't because they're not my cup of tea. But millions did. For a couple hours, her fans could read her stuff and they were happy. And EL James made a couple bucks. Good. We should all be so lucky.

Anyway, so I was all frustrated about that hack EL James (*shit!* Sorry, I take that back). I said to my wife something along the lines of "You know I should write the same story but with zombies. I could call it Fifty Shades of *Gray Matter*! GRAY MATTER, I say. Get it? Like brains because, you know, zombies. They eat 'em, so…"

Actually, if I'm honest, I was probably a bit slurry and far less concise. And there were likely some "fucks" in there.

Tiffany goes to me: "You should!" I laughed but then she said, "No really, do it. I dare you. It'd be hilarious!"

Me: Wait, if it's a dare… what do I get if I do it? (eyebrow raise)

Tiffany: If you finish it? How about you get a book that actually sells.

Me: …

[Note: There's a solid chance we weren't in a good place as a couple at that moment. But, in the end, that's neither here nor there]

So, I planned to write a zombie adaptation of the erotic novel but that satirical version… only got as far as the title. From there, the subconscious took over and the result was my five-part series *Fifty Shades of Gray Matter*, which had nothing at all, not remotely, to do with the EL James story.

Despite that, I ended up with a bit of a *Jekyll and Hyde* thing going on GoodReads about this book. Some gave me very low scores because they didn't like the rich spanky guy and his girlfriend (uh, not this book, but whatever). Others were angry because they wanted to read about Spanky but bought the wrong one, despite the **gauze and blood stains** on the cover of my book. Still others loved FSGM and hilariously mocked those who'd gotten it wrong (thank you Karla, you made me laugh out loud on several occasions).

One final note: I wrote this novel under the pen name Pat Connid, which is an anagram for "Don't Panic". At the time, I was working for CNN as a television producer for Don Lemon (and others). Back then, they frowned upon dalliances into supernatural fiction. Of late, it seems that's all changed.

So, to the thousands of you who've already supported this book, I thank you with all of my heart.

To my new readers— with a nod to my lovely wife and that one-time random over-prescription of Adderall for my narcolepsy— may I present to you:

The Swordsmen
(or Fifty Shades of Gray Matter)

a novel by

Dick Wybrow

Table of Contents

Pat Connid

Fifty Shades of Gray Matter

BOOK ONE

Let me be clear, gimpin' ain't easy.

Now, before you get your tattered knickers in a bunch, I want to say— right up front— you need to know what you're yourself getting into.

And let's be clear, yes, *you are getting yourself into it--* despite what others may have told you (the ones with working jaws and serviceable cerebral cortexes, that is), reading this is not required of you.

So, please, it's probably best you just go on gimpin' without any help from me.

This is simply a record of how I was able to stay, longer than most, cognizant, before ZBF (zombie bird flu) took me over completely.

This is NOT a handbook on how to avoid the onset of ZBF, nor is the procurement of said bundled wrap of soiled, bloodied pages a tacit agreement between you and me that I'll be any help to you at all.

Additionally, this isn't any type of guide of how one is to hitchhike across America, as a gimp, with expectations that one of the few remaining uninfected will give you a lift.

Why would they?

First, you'd be terribly difficult to get out of the upholstery. Second, the moment your tummy grumbled, you'd find yourself flung out the car at seventy miles an hour with red boot print in your hip.

So, get some good shoes. Because, face it:

Gimpin' is walkin'.

OH and don't get onto me about the "gimp" thing.

I didn't come up with it and if, by any sheer miracle, I survive ZBF I don't want those who feel they should take offense to my use of the word to *then* take legal action.

Or if, as expected, the court system collapses and the majority of our judicial stewards are splayed out across the country in lumps of zombie turds, I don't want instead those who take personal offense to me using "gimp"— because of *their* physical impairment— to arm themselves with fiery torches and chase me to the top of a mountain. However, if they did, I do take solace in the fact I'd likely outrun most of them. So there is that.

Okay, with that out of the way--

My best guess, the reason why I've lived this long is because of my total failure in trying to kill myself.

Oh, you may remember when ZBF first hit and how the world's scientists were dropping everything to come up with a cure and *blah blah blah*. And how all that panic turned to ecstasy after it was revealed that, *yes, yes!*, they'd incredibly found a cure for the blasted thing!

But before it could be properly distributed, reversing the looming human extinction, you may recall how that vaccine Innoc® got tied up in several fiery patent lawsuits— with warehouses of the shit just sitting in boxes as the lawyers hashed it out.

And sure, we've all seen the online news blurbs about

how the vaccine is "hovering at the edge of approval". If you missed them, they were usually a couple headlines down from stories about the latest retailer to get embroiled in a public policy fight and updates on the dwindling list of those to have not yet slept with Russell Brand (very often charitably broken down into "Men," "Women" and "Domesticated Other").

Part of the problem, it turns out— and I learned this through conversations over the past several weeks and months, held at various levels of intelligibility— is that some of the lawyers in the patent dispute themselves became infected but, as no one who knew them could actually tell the difference, the proceedings degenerated into an even more protracted trading of edicts and C&Ds and counterclaims until a majority of one group of attorneys sort of ate the other.

And, since it was understandably difficult to find replacement representation, as of this writing, the case is still "pending."

So, as a lot of us did, I grew a little down in the mouth about the whole humanity-coming-to-an-end thing. But, still, in the beginning I did my patriotic duty and went into work each morning, ducked the occasional *"rahhr!"* and gnashing teeth at the atrium's food court, and simply tried to get along with what was ever left of my life.

Ultimately, I think it was the traffic that got to me.

To be blunt, gimps can't drive.

And, I live in Atlanta where people here *started off* being really, really shitty drivers. And adding in the effects of ZBF— the blurred vision, inconsistent eye-hand coordination, and a cerebral cortex shriveled like Hitler's testicle on an Arctic expedition— and you've got a traffic jam that encircles the city, cuts through the city and clogs up most streets downtown.

Yet, while it was the 24/7 bumper-to-bumper traffic that put me over the edge, I can't ignore that it's *because* of the globe-wide traffic jams-- with zombied motorists honking, growling, giving whatever fingers that might be left to other zombie motorists—that's what has allowed the few remaining uninfected (a group yours truly is no longer a part of) to avoid, so far, being summarily attacked and eaten.

Many of *them*, the survivors, I understand, have gone to Canada. Via the surface roads, naturally.

Think of how that must have frustrated the Canadian tourism industry to no end! All those print ads and broadcast campaigns about skiing and fresh air and "darn good fishing"?

What a waste! Turns out, they had it all wrong.

Here's your big winner:

"Come to Canada. Zombies don't do winter."

So, then, what about those of us who are no longer pure human? We must ask ourselves, we who have begun "the turn," *What's our future like?*

Well, there isn't one.

That's the thought that led me to a local pharmacy, a drunk gimp seeking his way out. I was nearly undead and wanted to die.

Before being bitten by my girlfriend— and I should have known— my recent certificate of graduation from tech school in the city had put me on a good path to becoming a full-time graphic designer.

I was working long hours as a freelancer since, not yet full-time, the company could screw me out of health insurance and pay me a paltry hourly wage.

But, amid the fall of humankind as we know it, unemployment was high, so I was happy to have the job.

And, ultimately, the full-timers' Aetna plan didn't seem to cover zombification. At least not those who'd elected the HMO benefits.

One night, it'd taken me even longer than usual to manage the roads back to my home, weaving through the disaster-zone interstates— a rush hour clogged with zombied and non-zombied drivers (frankly, a difficult distinction to make in this city).

So tired from hours and hours on the road from a drive that used to take minutes, I'd decided on my way up to the apartment that I'd just put in my very last day of work.

No more.

Still, I was worried what my girlfriend would say. She'd lost her job months earlier and we relied on my income. But, mind made up, I threw open the door to my home ready to break the news— but *wow* was there a surprise waiting for me!

There's Millie... looking uncharastically sexy in the little nightie I picked up for her from a busted display case at a Second Chance store. All those times she'd rolled her eyes about putting it on, there she was that evening, lights low, soft music and wearing that little, faded purple nightie emblazoned with an angel on its front, which looked a little, disturbingly, like Dora the Explorer.

"Hey," I'd said, stuck at the doorway, unsure what to say next.

She smiled, walked to me and grabbed my shoulders, looked as though she were about to kiss me but instead, slipped down to her knees and with her eyes level with my belt, she began unbuttoning my jeans right in the doorway to our apartment.

"Hello," I said, not wanting to discourage her in any way. This wasn't something I'd often come home to.

Or *ever* experienced with Millie. Wasn't her "thing," as she'd tell me, usually scrunching up her nose while going on about her *alleged* peanut allergy. I didn't see the connection.

"Maybe we should go in--"

But, she ignored me, moving, prodding, unzipping and--

"WHATHAFU-HOLY-MUTH-jeez!" I said.

The first time my girl *ever* wanted to become an Atlanta Philharmonic first-chair flutist, and it's because she was hungry. Not wink-wink "hungry" but friggin' *real* hungry! As in, *Hal, I've become a zombie gimp while you were at work and want to eat you! Let's start with something small!*

Now, obviously, I survived the night. And, it's upsetting, because I really do miss her.

And I hated that she had to die, her skull bashed in with the figurines of a tin "frog band" her mother had given her the Christmas before. To remember my Millie, I still carry the little froggy tin banjo that had fallen from her split sinus cavity when she eventually crumpled to the floor.

She'd died, but not before-- of course— infecting me with ZBF.

I won't go into the details of the particular injury sustained, but I will say that when urinating, it's best for me to sit down lest I spray any nearby walls with a jerky, uneven output that resembles one of those *pftt-pftt-pftt* lawn sprinklers, several years beyond its warranty date.

There I sat that night, sipping the last of my beer, a bag of frozen peas in my lap, staring at my dead, gimp girlfriend... and, who was I kidding?

Even with the certificate, I wasn't going to have the great career I wanted. For one, it takes years and years to sharpen those skills. For two, the entire planet was infected with a zombie virus.

And, gimps don't need no logos.

So, that's why I ended up at the pharmacy down the street looking for as many painkillers as it took to kill myself.

SEE, I'VE NEVER BEEN the criminal type.

Not that I'm above it. And, I'm not passing judgment on anyone if they are the criminal type. Actually, I'm not really saying there is a criminal type, per se. You can't look at someone and say, "Whoa, that guy? Criminal."

Except, maybe, Australians.

They *were* criminals, right? It was some big criminal island for god sake. Like the "Island of Misfit Toys," except replace "toys" with words like killers, swindlers, bamboozlers and chronic parking violators.

But, if someone said I'd done something criminal, one look at me and really the only question would be whether I'd illegally downloaded *Stars Wars* movies or *Star Trek* movies.

So, a little B&E work? Not my thing.

And, in the dark street at one am, there weren't any Australians around to give me tips which, in the dark and alone, may have been for the best.

After a few minutes of "scouting" the building (I knew this much), I realized for the first time that breaking in is really, really hard. All those years, I'd *tsk-tsk* when catching the news about some dumb slob busting into some place, digging into the cash register only to find, duh, they didn't leave any cash in there overnight.

But, standing next to the CVS on Atlanta's east side, I realized those guys weren't dumb slobs, not one bit.

They'd gotten *in*, after all.

Sure, it hadn't often been a well thought out plan. Especially the guy that broke into a jewelry store, and got trapped shortly after realizing it was instead a candy store and, pissed, tried to eat all the candy he could before they cops showed up and put himself in a diabetic coma. Obviously, he hadn't been disciplined enough to conduct good, thorough research beforehand (or, maybe, just simply read the sign on the building). I blame the public school system.

First off, no way I was going to get through the front doors of the pharmacy. They were sliding glass but behind them was the lattice of an iron gate-- not getting in that way.

And, this surprised me-- glass? Not so fragile.

I'd always been so cautious with glassware because there's this impression that if it comes in contact with anything more solid than a wheat Triscuit, *smash!*

But glass, turns out, comes in different thicknesses. Yes, you probably knew that.

And the really thick glass, when you try and kick it, even when you try again and kick even harder, that shit sends a freight train of crackling-electric pain right up your leg that rounds the hard curve between the cheeks at Mach 7 and punches the spine like a steel-tipped sledge hammer.

"*Bwaaaaaaah,*" I said, rolling on the grass, clutching the back of my thigh with one hand while I rubbed my lower back with the other.

And, as I lay there in the dark, rocking back and forth, with the pain manifesting as bursts of light at the edge of my vision... it may have been a hallucination, but I swear a car whizzed just past my head and a voice called out, "Oy, mate, you're doing it all wrong."

But I can't be sure and, ultimately, it didn't matter.

Now, there are probably a lot of people who, if they'd been telling this story, they'd say that they got back up, shook off the pain, "sacked up," and tried yet again.

Screw that. It *hurt*. It *really hurt*.

As I lay there recovering, feeling the tingling effects of the virus begin to twinkle in my brain like baby fireflies, I had a newfound respect for the drunk, desolate hobos that had broken into places all those years.

Skill, my brother. Seriously, way to go. Sure, you may have oft pooped without taking off your pants, but... respect.

The night was getting a colder. And a dampness had begun to swell upon the soft blades of grass, which I'd fallen into weeping like a little bitch-man.

It would seem that just *deciding* to kill yourself, that would be the tough bit. But it takes, you know, work. Dedication. Stick-to-itiveness.

Determined, I slowly rose to my feet, catching a reflection of myself in the glass. I thought, *that guy can do it! Whatever it takes, me, I can figure it out.*

"There's a window above the back door that's usually open."

My head snapped toward the old woman's voice and, for a moment, my mouth hung open but nothing came out.

Where had she come from?

She looked to be near seventy, and dressed, impressively, in what looked like dozens of layers upon layers of clothing, most of which leaned toward the pink/purple shades.

She added: "Are you alright?"

I nodded quickly, not taking my eyes off her. Old, yes, but she'd come up on me like a ninja. Or I simply hadn't noticed. Either way, me no trustee ninja-granny.

Just behind her, there was a shopping cart overflowing with black garbage bags of stuff. There were various sizes of ink-black bundles, and I guessed (correctly, I discovered later) each bag held a different "type" of stuff. Maybe food or clothes or books or Tupperware, whatever-- each would have its own place with the others of its kind.

Under her left arm, she held a dog in a tight little doggie sweater. It may not have initially been tight but the dog, several days dead it seemed, had begun to bloat some— tongue lolling out, eyes bulging like Tori Spelling's botched boob job— and its garment began cutting into the pup's flesh a little.

"Uh, you see… It just, my inhaler--"

"The back. There's a window just above the far door," she said, softly petting her dead dog. Despite the gentleness of it, the creature's ear began to come a little loose.

"Yeah, they closed and--"

"What?" She looked into her cart for a moment, then back at me. "Oh, I don't care what you're doing. But, if you're going in and come across any chocolate," she said, smiling with tobacco stained teeth, "I wouldn't get mad if you brought me out some."

I looked around, flashing my eyes up and down the street, hoping no one was listening in as the criminal masterminds planned the big heist.

"Uh, yes. Sure," I said, walking toward the back, favoring the leg that gone up against the window and lost.

She called out after me, laughing a smoker's-laugh as she did: "You know they say that chocolate makes the same response in a woman that sex does?"

Eyeballing the doors at the back of the pharmacy, I muttered to myself, "Oh, so chocolate makes a woman turn over and pretend they're sleeping, *too*?"

My heart quickened, excited, as it seemed I may have

actually figured a way to break in after all. Well, not "figured" it out myself so much as a pink, homeless woman with a dead dog and a sweet-tooth simply told me how... but, splitting hairs, really.

SHE'D BEEN RIGHT ABOUT the window, and it had been surprisingly simple to get inside.

As I climbed in, my earlier admiration for homeless bandits waned a little. It seems there's a hobo intel network— they may just pass this sort of info along to each other. But, either way, didn't matter. Soon, I'd be filled to the neck with oxycodone, lortabs, percocet, hydrocodone, fentanyl and a handful of Rolos.

Hell, it was my last "meal," maybe two handfuls of Rolos.

Finally, once I got inside, it was clear why it had been so easy to break in.

The place was trashed.

Shelves stripped.

Ceiling tiles shredded, with conduit and wire dripping down like stalactites and frozen rain.

On the floor: food, wrappers, soda... and likely vomit and all the other liquids and near-liquids that come from the array of human dispenser points.

And, if I didn't find the drugs that would kill me the smell of the place might just do it. It was...
awful. So. So. Awful. Like a witch's sweaty taint after a midday bike ride. In August. On the equator.

My head swam. Sure, the room's aroma was getting to

me, but, I knew better. The effects of the ZBF were starting to take hold.

Walking slowly toward the pharmacy counter, easing my way through the darkness, my heart clutched in my chest— I was scared that my body and brain were changing.

How long would it take? Did I have seconds, minutes, hours? Would I know? Would I suffer? Would I still need to talc?

So little was known about ZBF— or, more correctly— very little on the news actually dealt with its effects.

Initially, we all remember the weekend specials and all the network morning shows showing up and broadcasting from Zombie Bird Flu outbreak flashpoints or the CDC right here in Atlanta.

However, after the "Matt Lauer Incident" (as it's known now), many of the networks bandied about the idea of tape delay to avoid scenes like that from making it to the TVs of the huddled masses.

But it went even beyond that.

In the end, corporate network attorneys convinced all the broadcasters to cease even discussing the effects of the disease, ostensibly trying to mitigate instances of FCC-backed obscenity lawsuits. However, it seemed more likely that nets were being threatened with rumored sponsor boycotts by civil activists who were "enraged and empowered by the negative, polemic characterization of our zombie electorate".

So, due to the subsequent singular nature of broadcast news coverage, all many of us knew about ZBF was the devastating psychological effects the virus would have on a couple's marriage. Or how difficult it was for a child living with the stigma in school, after losing a parent to it.

But how long it lasted, how it manifested and, of course, if the human race was indeed now coming to an end— this was never a topic of discussion.

So, climbing over the high pharmacy counter, the panic welling in my chest wasn't about falling, but anxiety about whether when my two feet landed on the other side of the counter, if I'd even be human anymore.

My brain felt like it was beginning to sizzle in my skull. And, there was a small ball of fire, there, just behind my rib cage (of course, this latter was just as likely just the smattering of heartburn I'd been dealing with most of the summer, lingering effects after our apartment complex held its annual barbeque social).

However, as I moved from shelf to shelf, slinking through the dark, pawing into each and every cubbyhole, my heart sank and my mouth ran dry.

Container after container: empty.

On the floor, there may have been a couple pills but those had been crushed underfoot. Shoe prints of pink, yellow and white powder.

Couldn't help it— a sobbing grew within me, my breath ragged but tears wouldn't come. I knew, despite the despair, the change was happening.

More shelves, more overturned containers.

Fighting off the sobs, I ran to the counter and searched beneath it. Pulling out drawers, tossing them to the ground, they'd shatter against the floor but, nothing. No pills to take me away from my zombie fate.

On the back wall of the pharmacy, I noticed there were a series of small sliding doors.

Pulling each down its track revealed only empty shelves, stickers, and hollow pill bottles by the thousands.

Then, a glimmer of hope!

On the far end, the final closet door had a keypad— and it had been locked.

Of course! They'd locked up their most valuable stash. And, despite some dents in the metal closet's door, it was intact.

The painkillers, if I could get to them, were right here! Just behind a locked cabinet door.

The keypad had been electronic— it was dead, no way to get in using that.

I spun quickly and grabbed the first thing in my sight. A stool.

The moment my hands gripped the rubber stoppers on its legs, they began to sweat. The effects of the virus were moving through me quickly, too quickly!

With all my strength, I prepared to hammer the stool down on the lock.

BLAM! BLAM! BLAM!

Again, I said it out loud, practicing the move in my mind: *"Blam, blam, blam!"*

In truth, I had no idea what it would sound like. *"Blam"* seemed about right, though.

Slamming it onto the lock (which sounded nothing like *"blam,"* by the way), the only damage being done was to my own shoulders, as they absorbed the shock from the metal-on-metal attack.

For the next ten minutes, I tried and tried and tried again-- but nothing. The thick metal would barely even dent.

My entire body, everything head-to-toe was drenched in sweat. This, either from the exertion, or it was my body, fighting, trying to hold onto those final threads of my humanity.

Just a matter of time.

In any moment, I'd be the Full Monty Zombie. And, it terrified me.

Surely, the will to end my life with some dignity would be replaced by the gut-wrenching hunger for living flesh. The only parts of me that would be human anymore would be whatever chunk I could sink my teeth into and pull from another person's body.

So, I cried.

I'm damn good at it. I can go full body, wailing, flailing cry, man. Not ashamed to admit it.

Because, in this case, when I did, I fell against the closet, then fell back-- inadvertently taking the closet with me.

Sobbing, my lips bubbling with spittle, and lying on the ground, feeling so sorry for myself, I realized I'd *taken the closet with me*. To the floor.

Eyesight blurred, I could faintly see the part on the wall where the metal closet had been— an area painted around in robin's egg blue.

I twisted, shifted, and got out from underneath the closet. And where it had been impenetrable to get in from the front, it had an open back that had been flush against the wall.

The tears now, were tears of joy, as I reached in grabbed handfuls of pills and chomped them. Momentarily, I choked, *whoa, yuk taste*... and found a half-drunk bottle of bubble gum flavored Pedialyte.

I washed down another handful of pain pills and triumphantly leaned against the wall as I sat, fist thrust in the air like Judd Nelson in the final frame of "The Breakfast Club," and his song became mine.

Don' chu….

The tears rolled down off my chin.

Noooo, don't go and forget-ting… meeee (admittedly, I never really knew the words)…

Don't, don't… chuuu!

It didn't take long. I could feel the effects of the drugs already seeping into my brain.

My racing heart began to slow.

My breathing, once ragged, now calmed. My chest no longer convulsing.

My head began to hum, and an odd tingling sensation flowed through me.

And, ultimately, that *last* bit... the tingling. That's the moment when I realized something was up, actually.

"It... what?" I said to myself.

Strangely, my head was clearing. The effects of the

Zombie Bird Flu, I began to realize, were actually
receding. But, it wasn't because I was dying.

At least, not yet.

Like a fever breaking, I could feel a part of my old self
return.

But, this blood-borne virus had retreated— at least in
part— from my brain because, it seemed apparent, a good
deal of blood had gone elsewhere.

My vision, now clear again, I scrambled back toward
the metal closet where moments earlier I'd eaten pills like
Pez candy.

Grabbing the main container I'd eaten from, I spun the
plastic jug around and leaned close to read its label in the dim
light.

"Cialis."

Blinking, I moaned, "Oh, hell no."

Then I looked at the other containers that had been
locked away.

"Viagra!" Another: "Levitra?!?"

Standing, wobbly to my feet, I looked down at the
"treasure" below me, in the metal closet. Unbelievable.

I yelled: "Of all the things they would put in a safe in a
city pharmacy *they locked up the boner drugs?*"

I'd taken several dozen tiny circles of blue and yellow
and pink (those may have been birth control, though)— and,
remarkably, it *had* staved off the effects, if temporarily, of
ZBF.

I'm not a doctor, but if I had to guess— and I could only
guess because all the doctors I knew had taken off to Canada,

despite their low-cost, socialized medicine— a fair amount of blood that had formerly been regulated to my brain was now responsible for the turgid, angry doom-stick that was raging just inside the zipper of my jeans.

Incredibly, it seemed, as long as the drugs were having this effect on my body-- the transfer of blood away from my brain-- even an amount this little (just being honest) was enough to slow the progression of the zombie virus.

I ran through the store, looking for something to carry it all in— occasionally banging Hal, jr. against a metal shelf as I did.

It'd seemed, incredibly, that I'd bought some time. I could hang onto my humanity for a little longer! And, coincidentally, I could also now hang dish towels on my body.

Returning with a small green knapsack, I stuffed all the ED medicine into the bag and climbed back outside the pharmacy.

My thought: I was in Atlanta. Home of the CDC. So, what the hell, maybe I had something? Maybe *this* could be part of the cure!

Well, I mean, not "this." *Private-Hal-reporting-for-duty* wouldn't be part of the cure, of course.

But, the ED medicine, maybe that was a key.

Slipping back out the window again, I dropped to the ground, banging "myself" on the metal door knob with a triumphant *clang!* I then cinched the knapsack tight to my back and stepped toward the north part of the city.

"Oh, hey, there?"

Oh jeez. Didn't even see her. Granny ninja was back.

"What," I said, spinning around. "I just--"

She stepped closer to me, eyes wide— "Did you find any chocolate? A lady loves her chocolate."

No.

No, I didn't.

And, sure, I'm not terribly proud of it, but I did now have, likely, the largest collection of ED medicine any one person on the planet possessed.

And, I know my goal now was to make it to the CDC and *Maybe Help Save Mankind*-- but employing this, the temporary "cure," was not without side its effects.

And, not all side effects are necessarily... bad.

I thought I'd be dead within a day or two, surely.

So, what the hell.

I put my soft hand to her wrinkled cheek and smiled.

"No, but I do have the next best thing," I said. "Why don't you put that dead dog down for a moment."

IT IS RATHER DISTRESSING to realize that your movies, for the most part, have lied to you.

I don't necessarily think there was any malice behind it. The filmmakers were simply setting out to make a couple bucks, most having left naive notions of "art" behind them ten minutes into Freshman orientation at NYU.

This, I was contemplating while walking toward the sprawling CDC complex that sits up in the northeast part of the city.

Up to that point, the walk had taken the better part of the night and half the next morning. Yet, still, I was totally awake and full of energy.

Sure, I was living in a sort of suspended animation—held in just that last second away from turning into Full Zombie. But, it a little like Robert Downey, Jr. in Iron Man—he's got that glowy, circle thing in his chest that holds back the bits of metal. If it turns off, the batteries run low or if it blows a fuse, then, *bam!* the bits hit his heart and he's dead.

My case was the same, if you were to replace Iron Man's glowy, circle thing with my turgid junk.

As long as that bit of blood was redirected, the ZBF couldn't turn my brain into a pink raisin. But there were other, new traits to being a near-zombie. Those I was just beginning to learn.

Two hours into my trek, I noticed that my vision had improved tremendously. Especially at night. Colors on the cooler end of the spectrum— the blues, purples— were crisper and clearer.

That wee benefit became especially apparent when I'd spotted a zombie straggler wandering in the bush— in the dark!— from a full quarter mile away. However, it had been my sharpened sense of smell that had picked up on the flesh-decaying fellow initially.

In fact, *that* had been one of the first senses to sharpen. And now you might say to me, "Ah, yes, like animal instincts. You can smell your prey in the wind now, Hal, can't you? Like some ancient hunter-gatherer. Nice. Man's new warrior breed, you have become."

But, I'd tell you right back, in a word: This place smells like shit.

I've discovered that the zombified sense most acute, most sharpened is my olfactory. And everything really, really stinks!

The city smells like vomit and poop and sweat.

The woods, they smell like animal vomit and poop and sweat.

Sure, I'd signed on to try and help save Earth as the zombie apocalypse was overtaking the human population, but *oh my god* the place smells like a cat's shitbox. All of it, with no escape!

And that's just slightly worse than learning my sense of hearing had also improved.

The good part: This helped me pick up on the *rahr, rarh, snarl* of that first woodland zombie I'd come across after my trip to the CVS.

The bad? I realized, after all these years: Coldplay really sucks.

All... this... time.

How could I be so wrong? Mulling this over, tears spilling from my eyes, I shook my fist to the freckled night sky-- *Dammit, Chris Martin. You charlatan. Snake oil salesman, stealer of hearts! You made me love you, so! Damn you!*

My tears had dried by the time I'd come close to the wood zombie, and he finally noticed me when I said, "Hey, wood zombie!"

Not sure why— maybe because my brain hadn't rotted out yet— but the Full Zombie folks didn't seem to share my heightened physical senses. OR if they did, they simply didn't give a rat's ass.

My appearance seemed to confuse the guy— he'd been a "guy" before this, or at least as far as I could tell.

The costume he'd been wearing when attacked was pretty ripped and over the past several weeks or months had become splattered in blood and gore.

Whereas, the face of man inside previously would have been covered by foam material, painted with a large comical grin and twisty mustache, *that* had been chewed away by the creature so it could get to whatever person it might be snacking upon.

Throwing caution to the wind after my embarrassment during the previous night's pharmacy window attack, I leapt forward and delivered an axe kick to the snarling thing's pirate shoulder.

I think it was a pirate. Getting closer, slamming a powerful fist into its solar plexus, I spotted a row of fake buttons and what looked to be some sort of ruffled collar.

It was only when I drove my fingers into its gullet, then pressed them through the tissue, up into its skull, pulling what was left of its brain out of the mouth, did I realize that this guy must have been one of those sidewalk wavers for a fast food chain. Given the piratey theme, it seemed Long John Silvers was near the top of the list.

Choking on its own blood and bubbling fluids, it's dull, yellowed eyes looked up at me from the ground, actually staring at its own brain in my hands.

"*Ugggrnggnfff,*" it said.

"No," I corrected. "I believe it's '*Arrrrrgh,*' right?"

Momentarily, I saw it gaze down away from my face. Downward, toward my belt.

Naturally, to stave off the zombie effects, I'd had to continue my regiment of ED medication. The moment I felt, uh, "the softness" coming on-- I re-dosed.

This, obviously meant, for my remaining days-- however few left there were-- there would be an angry trouser monster always accompanying me.

As the zombie gave it a long look, and I snapped my fingers.

"Uh, excuse me! Rude!" I snapped them again. "Eyes up here, please."

Choking, quickly fading toward death (you know, without a brain in its head, now), it gargled in its own blood: "*Agggnfffffntthh...*"

"It's '*Arrrrgh!*' you idiot," I said, shaking my head. "You must have been a horrible street pirate. Stupid. No wonder you're dead."

And with that, the light dimmed away entirely from its eyes and the pirate/zombie stopped moving.

That was my first encounter with a zombie, following my recent vocational digression (ie. Enemy of the Undead, Potential Savior of All Mankind, Ex-President of the Coldplay Street-Team-- Atlanta Chapter) and, as I'd dispensed with the creature, it was clear that my physical strength was growing.

On occasion, during my walk, I'd begun lifting things that looked heavy and was often very pleased with the results (as long as I didn't lift the much larger, questionable ones over my head-- picked up on that quickly).

My senses sharpened, the strength of ten men (to be fair: ten that probably didn't work out on a regular basis) and a determination to save the world. I was like a superhero!

An area just below my stomach ached slightly. I'd have to find some pants that were more... forgiving.

I was like a superhero, all right. A superhero with a handle.

Not sure what good that did, but we super-types all got our "thing," right?

SO AS I WAS saying about movies-- misleading.

It seems like a good moment to correct some misconceptions about zombies.

First, the whole "brains, brains, brains!" thing seems to really be off. Zombies don't care much about "gray matter"... and the use of that as a plot device-- or worse yet, using the phrase as some transparent marketing attempt to capitalize on the multi-million dollar commercial success of a content creator that an author might see as less deserving (ugh, *so* petty)-- is just an exercise in hackery.

Also, they don't necessarily move slow. They just got a bad rap, early on-- I'll explain that later.

One of the most important parts that movies never told us, as I've already laid out in some detail: Zombies can't drive.

Or rather, they can't drive well.

Now, that doesn't mean they *don't* drive. Far from it-- they seem to love it! Love it, love it.

You *may* be aware-- and if you're not, consider this then the only bit of advice in this writing (and, to be clear, that is not a legally binding statement)-- that generally, if you stay away from the roads and interstates, you can avoid the zombie hordes.

As I've said, in the case here in Atlanta, they've choked up all the interstates. Interstate 285, which circles the city in a loop sixty-four miles long crawls at a constant snail's pace-- day and night-- is absolutely loaded with angry zombie drivers.

So, actually, it's exactly as it was before the virus hit-- except the drivers smell marginally worse.

Rule of thumb for interstates: Steer clear (so to speak).

Now, I don't want to give you the impression there was some sort of "plan" in the making. At least, not for my part.

I was just a near-zombie guy with a knapsack full of boner medicine trying to make a difference in this big ol' world... but didn't really have a clear idea of how that would happen.

Slipping my phone from out a pocket-- it still had half a charge left-- Google Maps told me that after a night of walking, the CDC was still a good three and a half miles away.

And, for the most part, the city was going about its business semi-normal.

Which was why I felt perfectly comfortable going into the corner deli on Piedmont, across from the Atlanta Botanical Gardens.

My stomach had been growling-- I'd smelled the corned beef and provolone a mile back-- and since my consumption habits did not yet include the American consumer, a sammich seemed ideal.

It was late morning, so the lunch crowd had not yet shown up.

"Hey, wait! What ca--"

I raised my hands, then noticed the dried blood and goo and put them back down quickly.

Smiling, I said: "Don't worry. I'm harmless, just want a sandwich."

The girl behind the counter nodded slowly, the sun glinting off her steel nose ring. She looked to the back, then again at me. A small hand flew to her mouth, and she chewed on a chipped red nail.

"Uh, but..."

"I'm not one of them, seriously," I said, still smiling. "It's, you know, if I look like *this* they leave me alone."

"So, that's why--"

"Yeah, that's why the eyes are a bit yellow-- contacts, shhh!-- and, you know, the skin and nails are stained gray. That's costume make up. You can get it anywhere." I stepped toward the counter. "You know, you should actually consid--"

"Is *that* part of your disguise, then?"

I noticed she was looking through the glass of the display case. Down, beyond the deli meats to my... (too easy)... issue.

"Ah."

Her eyes flickered back up at me, then down again. "Does that, uh, ward them, off, too?"

I shifted slightly, moving my knapsack to my front. Sure, near-zombies can be modest, too.

"Don't worry," I said. "It's harmless."

"That's not what my mother used to tell me," she said and spit out a bit of nail.

The deli was small, only four tables, and I sat quietly as she made my sandwich. I'd had to settle with ice tea after first going with my usual Coke because-- *who knew?* --with my zombie-senses jacked to eleven, soda bubbles were razor-fucking-sharp.

The wonderful smell of the meats and cheeses had masked another-- chlorine bleach. Just behind that: secondary smell (or third, I suppose, if you were to count the bleach). One I'd become familiar with recently.

She was putting my food on a plate, when I asked:

"So was it one of them or one of us?"

"Was what?"

I stood and walked slowly from table to table until my eyes could pick up, almost invisible, little flecks of blood. Then, breathing in, I smelled the human bile.

"Did you kill them? Or did someone else?"

A heavy woman stepped out from the back, wearing a kerchief on her head; black, wooly ropes of hair sprouted from beneath it like a mop that should have been tossed out weeks earlier.

She wiped her hands, eyeballing me.

"Did who kill who?" She asked, climbing behind the counter and placing the new offering of sliced, smoked ham on top of an empty tray. A quick glance to the younger woman-- "You okay?"

"Yeah." Nosering shrugged. "Dude's just kinda weird."

"Hey!"

"Okay," the older woman said. "I'm just back there, remember. If the jagoff says or does--"

I interrupted: "HEY, I'm right here. You know I can hear--" I said, waving my hands-- "all of that talking about *me* because I'm standing two feet away!"

The woman with the sheep's hair looked toward me with a scowl, ready to fire some verbal missive my way. Her words got caught somewhere deep, though... and I traced her wandering gaze.

When I'd walked the length of the room, I'd left my knapsack back at my chair. So, at my waistline, for all the world to see, there was Hairy Hoodinky doing his Barbarian at the Gate routine.

"HEY, lady," I said, snapping my fingers by my ear. "Eyes up here. Rude!"

Nosering had placed the sandwich on my table then leaned up against the nearby wall. She looked tired.

"Don't you think it's odd that, it's like, we're all just acting like it's no big deal that those things are out there?" She wiped her mouth with the back of her hand.

I sighed and said, "It's how some of us deal with it, I suppose."

"Yeah," Nosering said, crossing her arms. "But shouldn't we all be finding some walled city or something? Hiding out until these... things... just all die off?" She pointed up to the television in the corner. The volume was off, the picture a little faded. "I mean for chrissake, it's the zombie apocalypse and Dr. Phil is still on the air!"

Glancing up and back, I said: "That's not Dr. Phil... is it?"

The older woman nodded.

"Yep."

"But... he looks, you know," I said to her. "Infected."

"He is. Got bit a few weeks back when they was doing some 'a zombie is my baby-daddy' episode--"

"He did a whole series on it," Nosering chimed in. "It was really, really good."

"But, then, I think it was-- like, what, Alison?-- a teen zombie baby-daddy or--"

"Nah, junkie-felon zombie baby-daddy," Nosering said, shaking her head. "Just up and bit Dr. Phil. The next day, he was one of those things."

I sat down, my head was swimming a little. Soon, I'd have to dose again. Or become like Dr. Phil.

That is: a zombie. Not, you know, a redneck TV shrink.

"Why do they have Dr. Phil in a cage," I said, not able to look at the screen anymore.

Nosering shrugged. "Some contractual thing where they can't call it Dr. Phil if he's not on the show. I licensing issue or something. So they wheel him out in the cage for at least two minutes a show."

"Seems a bit cruel."

"It's how Dr. Phil would have wanted it," she said and sighed.

"No, I really don't think so, actually." I said and took a bite out of my sandwich. "So, who died in here?" I nodded to the second table from the door. "Over there."

"Why do you think someone died?"

I smiled. Superhero cannot reveal too much about his secret identity. Although, as I thought of that... it was really my secret identity (which wasn't actually secret), worried about revealing my super stuff.

Whatever.

"I've always had a heightened sense of smell," I said grinning a bit too wide. "Like I can tell that, if you'll forgive me, one of you ladies is a little... aroused by my very presence here."

Listen, as I said. Taking the ED medicine keeps me healthy and non-zombie. But, obviously, one of the more aggressive side effects is I'm now always, uh, antsy.

The woman with the apron rolled her eyes at me and said: "First off, that ain't where a dead guy was. Some drunk college kid puked his guts out last night, and I had to spend forty-five minutes cleaning it."

Ah. I looked at the wall near the table. There was a bit of a flow to the faint stain. Yes. She may be correct on that one.

"And as for the other weirdo thing you said," Nosering said, pointing between her and the older woman. "We're married, Casanova."

"Oh."

"Yeah," she continued, on a roll now, "so nothing you've got-- especially *not* that 'hip stick'-- is going to rile up either of us."

The older woman laughed, then covered her mouth.

I smiled, inwardly. Alas, they couldn't know but my zombie super-sense simply could not be wrong about such matters!

"Ah, but I distinctly can detect, in the air, the unmistakable"-- I breathed in, deeply, through my nose-- "and delightful bouquet of a female in need, desirous for the touch of a male. Listen, you just wouldn't underst--"

From the back of the store, I heard at that very moment, most distressingly-- something go: *bark!*

"I have to leave," I said, grabbed my knapsack and sandwich, and exited the store.

AS I CLOSED IN on the Centers for Disease Control, I could hear far more commotion than I'd heard at any point earlier on the trek started the night before.

Mostly there were just various levels of growls, slurps, phlegmy roars.

Sprinkled in were the occasional "oh god, help!", "no, please don't, no!" and even a particularly strident "you never take me anywhere!"

For whatever reason, the undead had collected in pockets near the CDC. But getting through was necessary.

It wasn't much, but I had to bring the ED medicine to the world's premiere viral scientists. Maybe, *oh maybe!*, there might be something of a treatment or cure to stop the human race from being snuffed out.

And, if there were any cute girls there-- lady scientists, laboratory assistant girls, even a hair-netted cafeteria woman speckled with turkey gravy stains-- well, as I've said, I wouldn't have kicked them out of bed for eating crackers.

Christ, at that point, I wouldn't have kicked them out of bed for lighting fires.

One more advantage to being near-zombie. This, I learned with the CDC complex nearly in sight-- for the *most* part, the undead hordes didn't want to, in fact, eat me.

Certainly, my flesh had turned toward the zombie-side but not all the way. Still, to them it seemed I was a little like milk in the doorway of your fridge. You take a whiff and it smells *a little bit* off, it might be okay, but why chance it? Best to leave it for the roommate.

Or, another hungry zombie, as it were.

I'd learned about my exclusion from the zombie menu when coming across a middle-aged guy, battling three of them off with the leg of the one, it seemed, that was hopping. Impressively, Pogo Zombie was still on the feeding-frenzy offensive, but had a wee bit of a bounce in its attack, a spring in its homicidal step.

"Get awaaaay!" The chubby guy swung the leg hard, hitting one of his attackers in the head. Down goes zombie. Not bad.

Moments later, he was turned away from me and didn't see that the thing on the ground was slowly getting back to its feet.

Instinctively, I put my knapsack down and raced forward.

Chubbs yelled out, swinging at the two zombies: "Get.. .the fuck.. a-*waaaaaay!*"

The third quickly reached him and dug into his shoulder with a hand made of bone, sinew, and rotting flesh. The guy spun and raised the zombie leg, holding it by, what looked like, one half of a rather stylish pair of Doc Martens.

Then, catching sight of me as I ran to help, he hurled the leg in my direction, hitting me square in the chest.

"Ooof!"

The leg was heavy-- the fat guy must've worked out a bit.

From the ground, I lifted myself up on my elbows and yelled, "Dude, I'm on your side!"

His eyes were cranked wide as he tried fighting off three zombies, his fists and knees and elbows flailing in every direction.

Jumping to my feet, his screams rang in my ears, and I ran toward the huddle. Oddly, they suddenly looked like some zombie pastry, with the fat guy as a tasty whip-cream filling.

Oh no.

He cried out, "Help!"

I hesitated-- help him now and risk turning (thereby joining the other three in a midday snack) or quickly dosing and jumping in? There might just be time!

"*Ooowwww!*"

No, turns out, there wasn't.

My heart banging against my ribs, I ran to the knapsack, downed a handful of little blue diamonds and then ran back to see if anything could be done.

Now, it was just a writhing mass of bodies, but if I were going to be a candidate for Savior of All Mankind, I might as well start with the fat guy.

My two hands, rigid with my fingers pressed together, came down on the skull of the first undead diner-- splitting it on both sides-- and I lifted out the little, black-gray fist of a brain.

It went limp.

Reaching down, I grabbed the stringy hair of the second one and its mouth came open. As it glared at me with yellow eyes, I jammed my fingers up into its soft palate, grabbed me a handful of zombie thinkin' and yanked.

As it fell away, I could see the guy was still alive and fighting off the third one-- obviously the angriest since Chubbs had taken its leg.

"Get this-- *aaaaaooww*!-- get it off me!"

My heart sank.

The dude was alive but zombie bachelor number 3 had been munching on his arm (probably payback). Obviously, it had started at the hand, but that was gone, and was halfway up the forearm.

With a little less enthusiasm, I twisted the creatures head off from its body, tossed it aside.

The dude was writhing, bleeding, but his eyes were still wide and fierce. He put his hands up (well, *hand*) to cover his face in case I was just tossing the others aside to have him for myself.

Rolling back, off of him, I said: "No, no. I'm not one of them."

He was trembling-- either from fear or physical shock-- as he tried to form words.

Already, his skin began to gray.

"Dude, I'm so sor-- *hey!*"

What a moron I was-- I could start saving the human race with this guy after all!

Digging into my bag, I grabbed the yellow ones that were shaped a bit like a bullet.

I stuffed a half dozen into his mouth.

"Eat those! Quickly," I shouted.

He shook his head.

"Seriously, it's your only chance," I pleaded.

"No," he said, trembling. "I can't, I--"

Oh, he was so afraid!

"Just swallow them, you'll--"

"No, I can't," he cried out. "Can't dry swallow pills. They just get caught in my throat. Can't-- do you have water?"

My eyes darted in all directions-- I didn't see any water, but what I did see terrified me.

Coming at us, from all around us, hundreds of undead flesh-eaters.

It seemed they'd picked up on the scent of my bleeding, chubby new buddy.

I jumped up.

We were on a field of some sort-- like a football or soccer field. About a hundred feet away, I could see a soda machine that had fallen on its side.

"Hold on!"

As fast as my legs could move, I ran up to the machine and, then, tried prying into it. Not even when I tried my Terminator 2 hands, like steel judo hands, *hah-chaw! hah-chaw!*, could I get inside.

He began to choke and drown in his own blood and yelled, "Hurry, jeez, hurry!"

No time.

Stronger now than even a few hours earlier, I lifted up the Coke machine upright, grabbed its cord and searched around for an outlet.

Propped up against the wall: a rotting corpse. Or, rather, half of one. Shifting it to the side (*"pardon me, sorry"*), I found the plug-in.

Ding! The machine came to life!

"Yes!"

I dug into my pockets but came up short. Front, back. Nothing.

"Hey, man," I called over. "You got a quarter or nickel or anything?"

Unable to respond, he was gurgling and choking even more now.

Looking back to the corpse, it was the top half of a guy with a ball cap on. I dug into his shirt pocket.

Nothing.

Scanning the horizon, I sniffed the air and picked out its

particular decaying scent.

Then I saw it! I sprinted up to the other half of the corpse, only a few dozen yards away. In its pockets was a half roll of quarters!

Must have been laundry day.

Back to the machine, I dropped in the money, hit all the buttons until a can fell out.

I raced back to my struggling friend on the ground.

His eyes were lolling a bit in his head, but they brightened for a moment. I put another half dozen of pills in his mouth, popped open the can and held it to him.

Nearby, the snarling was getting louder. They were closing in on us, from every direction. It would only be--

"Can't! Drink.. it!"

I leaned in. "I'll help--"

"No, no," he handed the can back. "No diet. This is diet soda, I can't--"

"ARE YOU FUCKING JOKING, MAN?"

"No," he said, and barfed out a little blood, "I won't be able to swallow it. The taste is just so--"

As his words boiled into a coughing frenzy, I quickly ran back to the machine, dropped the remaining money in the slot and returned with another can.

As I held it to his parted lips he sipped... dribbling blood and Purple Fanta from his lips. Flecks of Cialis rode the oozing, drizzling stream like little yellow kayakers on a river of human goo.

His eyes flickered and closed, then he slumped in my arms.

"No, man," I said, apologizing in my thoughts, unable to say it out loud, unable to admit I'd failed him. "No, man, don't go."

How was I to save the human race, if I couldn't help one goddamn Chubbs?

Standing slowly, sadness penetrated my entire body.

It was such a deep, hollowing sorrow-- as if my heightened zombie senses weren't just limited to the five physical sensations. It was also my capacity to love. Incredibly-- as I wavered on the edge between human and undead-- my heart had never been so filled with love.

But, then I saw the hundreds of fucking zombies coming at me-- growling and snarling from every direction-- and knew, despite that, I'd be using the fat dude as a flesh baton to beat them all to death.

As I reached down for his feet to get a good grip--

"Wow, do I have a *wicked* chubby!"

I looked toward his face and saw his eyes were wide open! He was alive!

"Ya made it!"

"Hey man," he said, rolling to his feet. "You wouldn't believe--" He stopped mid-sentence and pointed toward my beltline. "Sick! You too? Dude, what did you do to me?"

"I saved your life, Chubbs," I said and he started to smile.

"Well, then, I appreciate that." Then he actually laughed.

Only about a hundred a feet away from us, moving faster now, the undead horde was closing in.

"Thing is, these ED pills may be a way to stop... all this," I said, rattled my knapsack, then strapped it tightly to my back. "We gotta get this stuff to the CDC. If it works on us-- it might be something that could lead to a cure."

My new pal, smiled again and shook his head.

"Sure, works for me," he said, then held up his arm. "Hey, I'm like a Vegas slot machine, man. One-armed bandit." He then blinked away some sudden joyful tears and nodded. "But you got me-- I'm in. I'll do what I can to help to you. To help everybody."

They were seconds away from encircling us, and we both readied ourselves for the fight.

But, while this grumbling, snarling mass of gimps were simply fighting for a snack, we were Fighting for the Survival Human Race!

I thought, *Two on two hundred? Bring it, gimp-fuckers!*

"What's your name?" I yelled out as we stood, back-to-back.

He laughed and said, "Well given my current and permanent state... I think Chubbs works just fine, man. What do I call you?"

"I'm Hal."

He roared with laughter-- he was gaining strength as I had and was feeling its intoxicating effects as it coursed through his entire body. Granted, it had a lotta coursing to do because he was a big fellah, but coursing, oh yes, coursing it did.

"Hal? That won't work!" He yelled over the growling that was growing louder and louder around us. "We are warriors for the human race, man. In fact," he said, and held out a fist, flipped up his thumb and pointed back at his groin. "We are bone-i-fied warriors for the entire human race!"

It was that moment, I knew.

Of course, he was right.

This wasn't just about living, surviving.

This... this was about fighting back.

Where now there were just two-- we could build a small army of fighters. An army of powerful warriors, the new champions of the human race!

And, yes, we are the ones you've heard about. The legends are true.

We are those warriors.

We are turgid.

We are The Swordsmen.

Pat Connid

Fifty
Shades
of
Gray Matter

BOOK TWO

"You should think about it," Chubbs said, smiling ear to ear. At that point, he'd been full on grinning for a full 20 minutes after our first run in with the zombie horde. Who can smile for 20 minutes? Dude's totally going to get wrinkles from that sort of thing.

It may not matter now that the human population was turning to zombie, but pride man pride!

We'd been quiet for a few minutes, both exhausted physically and emotionally, just walking along.

It seemed sort of a waste of time, but I couldn't help it-- don't like goo. So, as we walked along, I was picking out bits of shriveled muscle, chunks of meat-- I had this bit on my leg like a leech, so gross, for the longest time because I was staring at it just trying to work out what the hell it was. Turns out: bicep. Maybe a tongue. Yech-- and wiped blood off on trees and buildings.

Chubbs was altogether in his element. Now, as my second in command of The Swordsmen (unit members: 2), I was pleased with his performance at The Battle of Pop Warners Field #27. He did just fine.

From the surface-- and to hear him retell the story-- you'd think he'd won the damn battle single handedly for us. But it takes a strong command, right? Very, very important. If things aren't working at the top of the hierarchy, they turn to shit. Like Walmart. Old man Walton dies, his greedy parasitic prodgendy take over and the place is just ass. Ass with little shit-eating grin smilies everywhere.

So, as leader of The Swordsmen, I had to take credit for the defeats-- and the successes-- of the group. A terrible responsibility, but this is what I signed up for.

[quick recap here of first book]

"Hal, it wouldn't take anything man, it doesn't hurt," he-- still smiling-- held up both his arms. "You're already a bit shredded on both forearms, hack off the rest! Seriously, barely hurt me, man."

"NO," I said. "Like you were saying, right, we all got our own thing. You've got the Edward Choppyhands-thing and the singing thing--"

"Nope, not settled on one yet."

"Whatever, okay."

"But, I got good one for the time being, right?"

I shrugged. He laughed and I stopped him before he could belt out anymore of those horrible lyrics.

"No, seriously. Save it for the battlefield, man."

He clangged his new "hands" together and gave me a salute, which, not a good move, tore off a chunk of scalp, which landed on my shoulder.

Yech.

But, I had to give it to him, really I did.

When we'd first begun to take on the zombie horde at the Pop Warner Field battle, it wasn't going well.

The first few, weren't so bad-- I was doing my pincer Terminator 2 hands and going through skulls pretty good but found driving one down the gullet and up to the brain worked best. I was getting teeth marks around the wrist, though, I'd have to find some straps or something for protection.

But despite having the strength, killing gimps can really wipe you out. It's both aerobic and anaerobic. Same time. Hell of a workout. Maybe I needed a jogging suit (it'd help with Mr. Wigglesmith, certainly).

Chubbs was at a slight disadvantage because he'd had half his arm chewed off by those first three gimps. But, he was holding his own.

And, I learned, when this guy's in battle?.. chatter-box.

I first noticed the singing after I'd ripped the jaw off my fourth or fifth kill. It was a bit jarring.

"What are--" I said panting, turning my head slightly. "What are you doing?"

"...fiiigting!" He trilled out, then stopped. "Huh? I'm, oh, I'm singing."

"Why!?!"

A middle-aged gimp clutching a clipboard-- odd-- came at me moving at bit faster than the rest. I grabbed the clipboard and jammed it across the bridge of her nose. Gross.

Chubbs called back, "Used to be... a Rodeo Protection Athlete. It helped--"

"You what?"

"Rodeo Protection Athlete! We were there to help the guys on the broncs-- they go down--" he said and I heard him grunt, then a moist clicking sound, and a head flew just to my left, "and we gotta get in there and lure the bulls away and get the guys to safety."

I swung at paperclip zombie woman and caved her ear in.

"Rodeo Protec... you mean a Rodeo clown?"

"Well..."

"Rodeo clown, right?"

"Rodeo Protection Athlete-- only thing that stood between broncs and the riders," he said, panting. "But, yeah, sorta... Rodeo clown-like."

For a moment I was quiet as I finally reached in grabbed clipboard zombie-lady's brain and stripped it back out. Then, a little hesitantly, I asked:

"So like the shoes, and big red nose--"

"Yes, yes, yes! And fright wig, yes," he said, grunting as he fought off some sort of mall cop gimp. "But very serious bus--"

"The singing, then? Why are you singing Kung Fu Fighting?"

He yelled, then pushed one of the gimps to the ground, stomping its head and said: "It helps me keep a good rhythem. Was Rodeo Pro... when I was a rodeo clown, I'd run out and sing-- it seemed to calm the bull but mostly it was so I was on a rhythem. Easier to jump left or right, outta the way. Keeps you on your toes."

"Is it... is it helping the Kung Fu song?"

He let out a short cry. "I... I don't know. I'm-- aaaaaaa!"

"Chubbs!" I called out.

Again, the guys was in agony. He was down to just the one fist-- those gimps had eaten his left arm to the mid-point.

And, I got a quick glance, he had two chomping away at his right. By the time he finally broke away, he was now missing both hands, his flesh chewed up halfway up his forearm.

"I-- Hal, shit!" Spinning around, I sided up next to him. "What the hell am I supposed to do, now? I'm stumpy!"

"Just watch my back!" Two more were stumbling on the bodies around us, the ones we'd already put down, and I was battling them off.

"There's-- there's gotta be a hundred of these things. You won't be-- watch out!"

A big sumbitch came from my right and I didn't turn in time, his huge paw was coming for the side of my head. But the second before he connected, Chubbs was awesome-- threw himself at the big gimps legs took him down!

I saw him roll over a couple times then land next to a couple corpses-- gimps or people, they'd been dead for a long while. Wearing some sort of reflective outfits, they looked like school crossing guards.

He was slow to get up-- and I was still fighting off the two gimps and now the big fellah was getting back up.

"Come on man, need your help, here!"

He was almost balling. Snot coming down his nose, choking as he gasped, "Man, I got no hands! What am I supposed to do? I failed you, Hal."

"No, no! We're not out yet!"

"Failed you! I'm just--"

"Chubbs!" I yelled. "Snap out of it! Grab something."

"Dude, I don't have HANDS. 'Grabbing' ain't in my 'can-do' column anymore, man!"

That's when, I hit him. My heightened intellect and sheer will reached into Chubbs' heart and soul, and I dug my mind-claws into his man-stuff. Uh, into his psyche.

"Chubbs," I said, getting exhausted. "Your rider over here is getting tuckered out, man!"

His head raised, he looked toward me.

"Cowboy can only fight off these broncs so long, man." I ducked, slowly, got clipped.

"Hal!"

Stumbling back up to my feet, I said, "When a cowboy's in trouble... and, ugh, shit!.. that big ol' bull is staring him down. Gruntin' and huffin' and... dripping with gore and blood with a, looks like, a civil service uniform... could be a postal worker. Might be, maybe, a bailiff or something..."

"Wha?"

"Never mind, focus!" I said, and told him to get up. "Find something, rodeo clown! Find away to help-- ooooof! damn-- find a way to help protect your rider. Because I'm goin' down man. I'm goin' down, rodeo clown!"

I was going down, exhausted, beat. The two gimps were swiping at me and big fellah was now back on his feet.

Out of the corner of my eye-- I saw Chubbs, though, stiffen. He got to his feet and looked around.

Then it was like his entire body flexed like a muscle. He'd seen something on the ground, next to the two corpses.

Raising one arm, he plunged it into the ground and screamed so loud it spun the heads of my and the three zombies.

Another arm up, then down to the ground-- I saw this one clearer-- he'd smashed the bloodied stump of a forearm, like the other one before, down onto a short piece of wood.

He wobbled up to his feet, grinning like a madman. Smiling like a total lunatic.

Or like a rodeo clown.

"I got my fuckin' song, Hal!" He yelled and raised up and back, lifting his hands from the ground.

Extending from each arm, they weren't just sticks of wood. They'd belonged to the crossing guards.

"I got my sooooong, Hal! You ready gimps? You ready for Chubbs?!?"

From his arms, to the half fore-arm, down the pieces of wood, each arm was now capped with a red, octagonal, piece of metal and each of them had the word--

"STOP," Chubbs growled. "Hammer-time!"

"HOW DO YOU EVEN know the words to that horrible song?"

This made my little chubby buddy smile even wider, he started doing a little bobble steps, his dented and bloodied stop signs flashing through the air, splitting sunbeams into rails of light.

"My, my, my--"

"NO," I said, quickly looking around. "No, no, don't sing it. Uh, save it, you know--"

He nodded, feverishly, "Right, right."

"--for the battle, then. Not, you know... don't waste it..."

"Yep, gotcha."

"... out here where we don't have necessary ASCAP licensing."

"Sure-- what?"

I waved him away, "Nothing, just-- if you have to sing that song or any song, fine."

"It helps, right," he said and let out a whoop! "You saw how I brought the pain, baby!"

"Yes, yes," I nodded, trying to hide a smile. "Just let's refer to those songs in quiet reflection and not actually express the lyrics themselves vis-a-vis engaging in overt copyright infringement--"

"Song titles, that's fine, though?"

I nodded, stepping over a severed baby's arm clutching an apple. "Yes, yes. Titles are, happily, a gray area."

He was quiet for only a moment before the grin came back in full-force.

"You did pretty good, too, Hal."

"What? Yeah, well, I was also, remember, strategising on the battleground while you were, doing your spinny stop sign--"

"Ah-- Octx!"

"Yes, Octs, yes--"

"No, no. With an 'x,' it's Octx."

"Yes, fine, fine."

Chubbs had been quite good. A whirling dervish of a near-undead, former rodeo clown with two crossing guard stop si-- Octx-- stuffed down his forearms, slicing and dicing gimps in each direction.

Me, I was doing quite well, thank you, with the pincer-move.

Pinxer-move.

Pinzer-mauve.

No, whatever.

It's a bit like how dear Uncle Louie taught me how to find a woman's G-spot.

All those years back, seems like a lifetime ago, we'd be sitting out on the wrap-around porch of the home my grandfather built. Usually, it was late, most of the rest of the family had fallen asleep-- he and I weren't the sort that felt compelled to sleep our lives away.

We'd be out there, with the cicadas crackling their love-song in the moonlight, Uncle Louie'd tap his pipe out-- cashed another one, he might say and smile.

Then as he'd fill up his pipe again, he'd dig into his tobacco pouch and, there'd that smile, and, as he'd said so many times before, Louie would say, "This always feels like a vagina, this bit here. Soft, a bit damp."

I was seven and didn't really know what he was talking about. I wasn't yet a smoker.

But those totally inappropriate conversations of my youth would echo in my head as I slaughtered yet another undead gimp-- my uncle's words almost like instructions for how to put one down.

They were, of course, a verbal map on how to find a woman's G-spot-- but they served me far, far better as a path on ripping a gimp's brain out of its skull.

"Ya go in, up to th' hilt," he say, his hand grinding into the tobacco pouch far longer than necessary. "Arc up like you're sayin 'Hey, come 'ere, darlin'. Come 'ere."

Yep, that was my move. Come here, darlin'. Then I strip the brain from the top of the spinal column and pull it out through the soft palate.

Funny, all those years armed with that knowledge, it did fuck-all for me when trying to find the G-spot.

But damn good for zombie killing.

As I walked in the midday sun, heading toward the CDC-- we were nearly there, about a quarter mile away now-- I wondered if Uncle Louie was still around or if he'd gotten bit and turned gimp.

We sort of lost touch in the years after he moved a ways out of town.

Every few months he'd call and say something like, "Hey, why don' chu grab a bunch a quarters and we'll go see some movies!"

But, my mother would get on the phone and that would be the end of that.

And since my family lived within 2000 yards of a public school, Uncle Louie couldn't risk violating the court order, so I didn't see much of him in my later childhood.

My eyes watered a little as I thought, Uncle Louie was a little bit like my Mr. Miyagi. Right? See, I think I'm learning about G-spots but no, no. Ha! Uncle, he was teaching me how to survive an undead apocalypse and didn't even know it!

Amazing.

And, funny now I think about it, like Mr. Miyagi, he had a whole "wax on/wax off" thing, but I'm pretty sure that was exactly what he intended it to be and nothing whatsoever like the movie at all. Nothing I'm emotionally strong enough to repeat, frankly, so I'll end that little digression right there.

Now, it hadn't been a total shock, I suppose as we'd come over the ridge.

Me and Chubbs hadn't talked about it, but as we drew closer to the CDC, there were fewer and fewer words between us.

Like me, his heightened near-zombie senses picked up on the quiet-- and the smell of burnt government paperwork and red tape. And the bodies. That was the really gross bit.

The campus has-- or had-- a central complex, staff and visitor housing, library facilities and an a museum.

If it had been able to boast an affiliated amatuer sports franchise, it may have even been mistaken for a small university. Of course, given that it is, in fact, the Centers for Disease Control, my guess is that organized gaming events would present an attendance challenge, and any type of confectionary at the "snack shack" would find itself, week after week, disappointingly unsold.

As we came up through some bush to a set of railroad tracks. The parking lot of the CDC was just beyond the tracks and it was a mess.

Bodies, overturned cars, burnt out machinery, burning barrels...

Chubbs sighed, his grin finally faded.

I said, "Burning barrels."

"Huh? Yeah, awful, huh?"

"Sure, but where'd the damn barrels come from?"

"They... I dunno. They probably had, you know, stuff in them, man."

I stepped over a track and looked down. Something had caught my eye.

"Yeah," I said. "But anytime you've got like a situation where shits just all tore up and like there's been a fire-fight or something, there's always these burning barrels around."

"Huh. Yeah, I suppose."

Bending down, I added, "I mean, I bet you if you looked around this place ten minutes before-- you know... whatever chaos, whatever the hell happened here-- you wouldn't see a damn barrel anywhere."

Chubbs caught sight of what I'd picked up and smiled again.

"But, bam!, all hell breaks loose and when the smoke clears-- well, the smoke doesn't damn well clear because you got the friggin' burning barrels that come outta nowhere."

"Hey," he said. "Spike! Cool."

Two tracks formed a "V" in front of us, become one just to the west. Right at the elbow (or if you were more vulgar (and probably are, nasty) you might say, right at the "crotch") there was a build of of gravel, bits of metal and a rusted railroad spike that had come loose.

My new sidekick spotted another a few feet away.

"Hey!"

He ran over and realized that, with his new "hands", his Octx, he was now down two opposable thumbs. And, well, all of his fingers.

Enthusiasm refusing to wane, he walked around the spike a couple times until he decided to give it a flick up in my direction.

And, I have to hand it to him (because he certainly couldn't hand it to me! Bah! What? Nevermind), for a big fellah, he's got some natural athletic ability.

"Shit, sorry man."

Now, his problem solving skills are, as it were, hit and miss. This was never more apparent than after "flicking" the five pound rail road spike and hitting me square in the chest.

"Does it hurt?"

"Ugh, yeah it hurts, you sunk a spike into my chest man!"

I stared at it and then the one in my hand. These would be a bit of an upgrade from my pincer-fists (which always ensured a good half hour of serious, serious cleaning under the nails) and, given that the one he tossed my way sunk as deep as it did-- they'd do well for some gimp killin'.

When I looked up, Chubbs was quite, looking down at his hands. Odd but for some reason I knew what he was thinking.

It had occurred to me at the same time.

The spike sticking out of my chest. And, as an aside, a permanent raging hard on about eighteen inches below it. In silhouette I looked like half a coat rack. But that's not what struck me.

"You think we can die, Hal?"

"If I do, Chubbs... I'm doing it while pulling out the brains of as many gimps as I can."

He nodded, smiling again.

As I reached up to pull the spike from my chest, he yelled out: "No! Wait, don't do that."

"Why? I'm not really going to bleed much-- I'm near-zombie, man, it'll just--"

"Naw, I mean... it looks kinda bad-ass!"

This guy.

"Seriously," he added. "Dude, you've got a railroad spike sticking out of your chest. I knew people who that they were bad motor scooters because they had a safety pin in their nipple-- you've got a railroad spike sticking out of your chest."

"Huh. Well..."

"You look like a dude not to be messed with!"

I shrugged, turned sideways and gave him my silhouette view. "Or a dude to play ring-toss on."

Chubbs laughed and started toward the CDC building.

"Hey," I said walking next to him. "You never said why you were in that field, by the way. First time I saw you."

"Oh that," he said, eyeballing the huge complex. Not a single car moved, there were no lights in the windows. Place looked either dead or dying. "Just over that way about a block or two, there's a seniors home."

"They dropped a nursing home next to the United States' complex holding the most virulent and deadly diseases on the planet?"

"Sure," he said, stopping and pointing with his left Octx. "The real estate they got real cheap."

"You think?"

For a moment, something seemed to drift over his face, then he said: "Before we give this place a try, you mind if we head over there?"

"But you were already there, weren't you?"

"Nah, I was trying to get over there but the roads were all choked up. Horrible traffic and--"

"Yeah, gotcha."

"So, I parked up the way and tried to cross from back here."

A glance at the CDC and I knew that it wouldn't be as simple as knocking on the door or ringing a bell or setting a barrel on fire (maybe that's what they were for??). Half hour at the old folks home might be a nice, quick rest for whatever other challenge lay ahead of us.

"Oh, no, it's completely overrun by undead."

I stopped, flipped the spike in my hand a couple times, then pocketed it. For now, sure, I left the other in the middle of my chest. Because taking it out, there'd be a big hole and my shirt would be all tore up and, I guess, a little bit it did look kinda cool. A little.

"Uh, then why do you want to go there?

"There's a pretty good cafeteria-- we can get some food." He saw my expression and then laughed, "Oh, those ones, they're no big deal. They were some of the first."

"First what?"

"The old folks over there. At least here in Atlanta, that was where they first sprung up."

A quick glance to my right-- big building full of viruses. A glance ahead-- this is where we first see zombies. Hmm. Might be a connection (duh, yeah? You fucking think so?).

Picking up the pace a little, he told me what he knew of it.

Apparently-- and a lot of this was speculation, but this guy he knew told him, so it seemed pretty legit-- some at the CDC was experimenting with two particular types of drugs. In fact, it's believed that it wasn't just the CDC-- the FBI and the CIA were both involved.

When some concerns were raised by the oldsters, many noticed that suddenly they were getting new pills, then the AARP got involved.

"But," Chubbs said, "The AARP, they were in on it. Paid off, right? So, despite promises, no help there."

Concerns were raised with the local chapter of the National Institutes of Health but when the NIH reached out to the CDC, the DHS threw up roadblocks saying it was a national security issue.

"So they were S.O.L."

"What's S--"

"Shit outta luck."

According to the guy who told Chubbs, no one knew where it started but as far as anyone could cobble it together, it was rooted in FEMA.

We were headed up a road toward the nursing home. Huge chunks had been carved out and there were a handful of cars, burnt out and overturned, some had slid and were askew in holes blown out of the roads.

"Shelling. All up and down here."

"When?"

"Weeks ago," Chubbs said as he kept his eye on a couple of slumped gimp bodies. "FEMA agents. Or so everyone thought."

There had been some partnership between the DEA and the CDC, backed by the FBI, secretly facilitated by the NIH, cheered on by the DHS with catering by FEMA.

"What?"

"Yeah, you know those little MRE things they give out for disaster victims and shit?"

"Those don't look very good."

"Actually, you look for the blue packets. Fruit-tasting. Not bad."

"Good to know."

It turns out after going through years of animal testing, the FDA quietly gave the nod to a program to test these new drugs on people. But secretly. So, how do you give huge groups of people pills in secret? Find a group that already takes a boatload of pills and slip 'em in.

As he explain it, we came onto the nursing home.

It ruined, windows bashed out, bodies torn in pieces, scattered across the lawn and--

"Look!"

"See, I told you," I said, staring at the burning barrels. "All the time!"

"Yep," Chubbs said and lifted his Octx.

He'd heard it, too. And I'd certainly smelled them back when we turned down the road. Where the CDC looked dead, this place was undead. Crawling with gimps.

We weren't going in the front door-- with the windows smashed out, I'd seen a couple pass by the front desk already.

He knew, of course, other ways inside.

"You think we should be doing this? If we get trapped, Chubbs..."

"These are gimps but they're old shuffleboard-playing and Murder-She-Wrote-watching gimps," he said, his voice lowered a little. "They're still kinda deadly but they move real slow, right?"

"Of course. Right," I said and nodded. These were some of the first undeadies to wander the streets. The very first. That's why gimps got the bad rap for moving really slow. They were zombies, sure-- they were just really, really old friggin' zombies.

Like nana zombies and poppy zombies.

Nana zombie would probably bite you, then come at you with a kleenex... try and dab it with spit and wipe off the blood. Yech. Nana spittle.

Not sure if Chubbs was on the same progression as me, as near-zombie senses go, but I'd have given away my entire catalog of Men at Work CDs (many of them signed, by the way. Jealous?) to not have such a good smeller.

Dead rotting flesh is an awful, putrid that seems to only get worse the more you breath in. Add in the smells of the city-- garbage, sewer processing, Sabrett hot dog carts-- it's nearly unbearable.

But nothing compares to breathing in bits of old people.

This thought hung with me, a little too long, as Chubbs got into his fight mode and slowly walked a line of bushes to a door around the west side of the building we were heading for.

He stopped, spun around to me and whispered as we approached a husk of a body, mangled and twisted.

"Oh, hey, I know that girl!" He said, stepping over what was left of her right foot (which was about a yard away from the rest of her body). "Worked in the gift shop. Used to rip off everybody."

"Woah," I said catching sight of her face. Or, rather, where it had been.

"Yeah, they were probably happy to eat her," he said, still whispering. Then giggled a little. "Dude, it was like a refund!"

"Okay, yes. Keep moving. Smells horrific."

And it did. Because-- and this thought I could never quite shake from my mind-- all smells are "particulate." This I learned from my eighth grade Earth Science teacher, Mr. Jepson.

"What does that mean?" Some brown noser had asked, dooming him for a beating after class.

"It means that the receptors in your nasal cavity, they work by sending message to the brain," Jepson answered, in anticipation I'm sure, of the 'holy shit' hammer he was about to bring down on all us kids.

"So?" said the brace-faced teen brunette, a sweet girl who'd years later dropped out of the local community college after unknowingly being films and subsequently featured in a YouTube video involving a third of a bottle of tequila and a half dozen ping pong balls.

I understand she's very popular in Japan, however.

Jepson told the class: "It means anything you smell-- that's a part of what you're smelling, lodged into your nose. If you smell roast chicken, that means microscopic bits of roast chicken had floated through the air and sunk into the olfactory receptors."

He waited, watching the class, the smallest of odd (read: evil) grins on his face as it all sunk in.

"So," Timmy Phillips had said, essentially, what we were all thinking, "Whereas the first who smelt it dealt it-- it seems that all who smelt it have shit in their nose."

While he was correct, certainly (horrifically!), it took him several weeks to recover after Mr. Jepson, not a fan of such colorful language, split his bottom lip with a ruler thrown from across the room.

The truth may set you free-- but it may also get you talking like the "Heyba, manba" guy from the Cosby Kids if you don't watch yourself.

However, that thought-- the smelly particulates-- was front and center as I breathed in, smelling all giant mass of undead old people: the stench of sweat and sloughed off skin and dried pudding and Bengay. All that, microscopic particles, were in my noggin.

Needed to be sick. Urp. No time.

"Okay," Chubbs' yellowed near-zombie eyes were almost sparkling as he told me his master plan: "I have no plan."

"What?"

"You're the general here," he said, inexplicably grinning again. "I'm playing it by ear, man. You got a plan?"

"No," I said stepping back and look up and down the building. Taking in the surroundings and coming up with fuck all. "What... I mean, where--"

"Oh, yeah," he said finally. "I work here. Or, I did."

"They need rodeo clowns for nursing homes?? The hell did you people do--?"

"No, no, no," he said and cracked the door open, sending a lighting bolt of terror up my legs, across my thighs, clipping the tip of my boner and landing in the pit of my stomach. "Not a lot of work for that lately. I came here. Worked part-time as an orderly."

"Oh, that-- wait, don't open it up yet!"

"Don't worry, they move slow," he said. "These folks were ancient before they were undead."

And with that, the crazy bastard slipped inside.

The door bounced on its jamb for a moment and I waited to hear a crunch, "aaaah!" from the other side but nothing came. However, in the distance, outside I could now hear them, wandering the grounds.

Quickly, I slipped inside.

"Dude," I whispered-yelled as my eyes got used to the dim light."

"What? Hurry up."

He was already about twenty feet down the hall and I could hear them everywhere, munching and gurgling and growling and slurping. I did not want to be in a zombie old folks home, not one bit.

My legs were shaking a little, my feet sliding along the floor which was slick and sticky at the same time.

"Jeez, why are we even in here?"

Chubbs didn't look back as he tapped one of his Octx up on the sign just above his head. The loud metal clank of it was startling, and I think a tiny bit of poop came out of me.

Seriously, I had to get it together. The leader of The Swordsman must be brave! And, of course, I had be an inspiration to my men, err, man as they head into battle!

Yes. As Lord Nelson, I believe, once said as he led his men into the Battle of Copenhagen, "Gentlemen. I believe it is time to sack up."

Looking ahead, my friend had come across a gimp in a walker. Chubbs just looked back to me, shrugged, and went around it.

Then the thing took a bite of his ass.

"Heeyy!" he screamed, and spun away. The geezer gimp fell back a little, its teeth still in Chubbs' flesh. "Jeez, get 'em out, get 'em out."

I ran forward, keeping an eye on my left and right-- I saw Jurassic Park: Don't want no gimps coming at me sideways in some geezer gimp trap!

The thing was on the floor, it's hands, mostly bone and sinew and yellowed nails, were gripping into his calf. It seemed to catch sight of its false teeth dug into Chubbs and reached up.

"No ya don't!" I yelled at it and drove the railroad spike in my hand down into his wrist.

Chubbs, balanced against the wall, yelled too, "Actually, yes, please get the teeth out of my ass, man!"

"HOLD ON!" Down to one knee, I pulled the spike from my chest and drove it into what brain it had left. The geezer gimp went limp.

"Ow, that hurt."

Pulling the teeth out and tossing them aside, I said: "Thought you said they were slow."

"Yeah," he said, rubbing his backside with a stop sign, "But they're sneaky, right? Ow, hurts like hell."

I looked back to where we'd come to see if there were any more that way-- not yet.

Only thing moving was the sign Chubbs had tapped a minute earlier. It read: Cafeteria.

"Okay, let's get some food and get outta here."

FOR THE MOST PART, he'd had it right.

When we'd come across an oldster, for the most part, a quick whack and they were down. Not much of a threat, ultimately.

Still, the place was dark, creepy and with a lot of weird cubbies and corners.

And the smell, of course, but I mentioned that at length already. Just wanted to say though-- still very blechy.

"Why'd you work here?" I asked him. We were about fifty feet down from the cafeteria, but both he and I could hear the geezer zombie sounds pick up. Seemed like more of them down that way.

"My father was here. Gave me a chance to be nearby."

I stopped.

"Oh, man," I said. "You didn't say your father was one of these things." Couldn't help it, my voice caught a little in my throat. "It... I'm so sorry, man."

"It's okay. He's a tough ol' guy."

"I see. You're worried he's suffering like this."

Chubbs turned his face away for a couple seconds and then said, "Let's just get to the cafeteria, man. Get our grub and get out."

For a moment, my heart really ached for the guy. My father had died when I was very young-- killed in an odd mishap with a Black & Decker hand vac no one would fully explain to me. So, me, I knew about death, sure.

Trying to cheer him up, I picked up the conversation: "Maybe there's a couple bags in there or something. Duffle bags and we can load up with food for a couple days. This was a good call man," I said and he returned a smile to me. Good.

"Yeah?"

"Yeah, and these things aren't so tough, like you said. Hardly a threat, right?"

"No, not really," he said, as he flung the doors of the cafeteria open. "Unless you got a lot of them all at once. Then--"

He stopped, staring into a sea of creatures.

Writhing of bodies, half in and half out of their hospital gowns, rotting limbs, diapers full to the brim... it was geezer zombie central!

And when we'd flung the doors open, all their yellowed, blood flecked eyes turned toward us.

I'D DONE A LITTLE running in my current state, ie. with an erection hard enough to crack spanish floor tiles.

But, still, it was a challenge.

And, I had to help my partner because he was still trying to get the hang of his Octx, as he pumped his arms to run. Coupled with the fact the spot on his butt hurt from the run in with Capt'n Chompers, he was a moving a bit slower than one would hope when being chased down the winding hallways of a dark, damp nursing home with a couple hundred geezer zombies drooling and slurping behind you and, surprisingly, running at a pretty good clip.

"Which way?"

Chubbs looked up and around.

"Too dark..."

Then he looked back at the housecoat zombie hoard behind us and sprinted forward, leaving me a little flat-footed.

Catching up to him, we rounded another corner. Above us, ahead, just barely swaying, was a sign that read: Cafeteria.

"Oh jeez, man!"

"Sorry, it's hard to see-- I never come around here before when it's so dark and there's weird goop on the floor."

"We're right back where we started!" Which, I realized, meant the exit was just-- I spun around and could see the door, still cracked open slightly, a thin beam of brilliant beautiful light spilling onto the floor.

"Look, we can--"

Arms and legs and even tongues flapping, the geezer horde rounded the corner, moving fast, blocking the exit.

"No, we can't."

Behind us, a voice called out.

"Hey! HEY."

In the light, we could barely see him, but it was one of the residents of the home-- not yet turned full zombie.

And, I say full-zombie because, as we got closer, we both could see he was near-zombie like us.

In every way.

"That was you guys? That's why they left?" he said, as we came up. "I was trapped in the cafeteria for five days eating nothing but canned meats."

"Ughhh," Chubbs said and I had to agree with him.

"Arrrgh," the approaching geezer zombie horde said and we had to run again.

The old guy knew the place better than my second in command, so we followed him. And, of course, neither of us could help but notice. When the guy saw what we were staring at, he pointed to his arm, lifted his sleeve.

"Yeah," he said. "I'm on the patch." Then he saw our similar conditions. "HEY, you guys, too?"

No. No, mine wasn't anything like the petrified forest wood gramps had, no. Nothing like--

"Yeah, us too," Chubbs said. "No patch. We got pills."

The three of us climbed up a set of stairs as we both explained to the old guy that it was our turgidness, that was what was keeping us from going full on zombie. For whatever reason, this thousand year-old guy (okay, not that old) was taking ED medicine! Must have been the local ladies man.

"No, they gave it to me," he said as we reached the floor above. Brighter up there, we could see several exits, each clear of any geezer gimps.

I asked: "Why would they give it to--"

"Hey, where are you going?"

Chubbs had turned toward the big double doors at the front-- the ones we'd seen smashed out earlier. The old guy was shuffling along in the opposite direction from the two of us.

I called out, "We gotta go, man."

"Not without my rascal," he said, looked back at us and kept moving. "I don't move so well, I need my scooter!"

Looking at Chubbs, he looked at me.

Here was the first non-gimp we'd come across, but how the hell could we drag him along in our Quest to Save All Humanity Even Those Who Didn't Deserve It?

Our decision was made for us when the geezer zombies started spilling up the steps, the first wave crawling, choking on their own blood, gasping for breath as others brutally clambered over top of them, crushing some of those below them into stomped piles of flesh.

This huge, squirming mass of rotting bodies now was between us and the old guy. Ah well. He was toast.

We had our way out.

"Oh, shit," Chubbs said.

Between us and the door was one old-- but big-- geezer. Strong, mean looking and--

"My dad."

"What?"

My partner turned to me, looked back at the geezers getting up the steps, regaining their footing. As serious as I'd ever seen him, he said:

"I gotta do this."

I looked down the hall where his father was blocking the door. Growling, slurping, arms flailing like tentacles.

A glance back at the mass of geezer zombies-- whoa. I had to take on that while he got some goddamn closure with his dad??

"Listen, why don't we--"

"Hal, man. I've never asked for anything."

"Well, yeah, I've only known you for about an hour. Hasn't been much time for that, has there?"

With that he walked slowly toward his father, his shoulders slumping.

I readied myself as they oozed toward me. Stinking and chomping, slinking down the hall. Some on their knees, some hooked over as they walked, making these guttural, disgusting noises as they're mouths--

"You mother-fucker!"

Fingers digging into the floor, into each other, oozing--

"Oh, no don't you run away, hell no, bitch!"

And each of hungry, each of them wantin--

"Yeah! That's what I'm saying!"

So, I turned around for a moment to look at how Chubbs was dealing this the tradegy of having to take his father's life.

"Bam, another to the face, bitch!"

He was coping well.

"Why.." he yelled, kicking out the big undead geezer's legs, "didn't you..." he stepped onto things chest and drove an Octx down, splitting one of its arms off like a wishbone, "just let me do..." crackkk! "... what I wanted to do?"

I called out, "You, uh, you all right, man?"

"Naaaww!" Chubbs yelled, but not to me. "You wanted to me to be a rodeo clown?" Slice, gash, rippp! "Who the fuck wants their kid to be a goddamn rodeo clown?!?"

Clank!

"Twisted..."

Chink-squish!

"crazy..."

Glat-glat-glurp-bwop!

"old motherfucker!"

Grief, pain's unforgiving mistress. Sad.

I spun back around just as the first several of the gaping, toothless, bloodied maws came within inches of me, and jumped back, slipping on fluid and blood and rice pudding or something, falling back.

"Ow!"

They towered over me now, leaning down-- face after face after face filling my vision, growing larger, hungrier.

Trying to scuttle back on my elbows, I made a little way but not enough: one of them on the bottom, its head twisted back under the pressure of the others, had grabbed my foot and was pulling me into the geezer zombie horde.

"Mrrrannnnrrrnnn!" one of them, the nearest, was inches from my face but I couldn't break away. It felt like I was being sucked into them.

Then, I remembered: the spikes!

Earlier, I'd stuffed them down into my pockets and with my right hand was able to pull one of them out, jamming it into the ear of the closest one. It's head split, gore and blood and, likely, rice pudding, split down onto my chest.

"Chubbs!"

Arching my head back, I called again-- "Chub--"

He was already on them, his dear ol' dad just a clump of pulverized meat at the door.

His Octx flailing, he cut the closest ones from me away and I lifted myself from the creature that had my foot, freeing it, only to have another to grab hold, uh, elsewhere.

"Holy, mother-of-!"

"I got it!" Chubbs yelled out and raised back his left battered and bloodied sign.

"Whoa-whoa-whoa! Be careful man, cut the gimp, not Hal, jr. and-- OOOWWwww! Dude, hurry!"

He sliced in but the of geezer zombies pressed back, moving in, trying to devour the two of us. Chubbs tried to pull back and hit it again but--

"It's stuck, man," he shouted, true fear in his eyes, "Can you wriggle it?"

"What? No, get them off, get them off!"

"Wriggle, man," he shouted, turning strident, "Wriggle it, man!"

But nothing I could do was loosening their grip-- our only defense was Chubbs' other Octx, as he sliced and cut and swiped at them, keeping them at bay.

The reality sunk in-- there were dozens, maybe a hundred of them. No way Chubbs would be able to put them all down without the things devouring us first.

"I just wanted to say, man," I shouted. "You, you were really great."

"What? Hold on!"

"Yeah, no, but we would have made a good team."

Chubbs' face turned red, his eyes blazing, "We are The Swordsmen, General! I will not let them take you!"

Slowly, I was being pulled under; only his right arm free, holding them back.

Bulging, gurgling they seemed to grow larger before us.

Breathing heavy, he yelled, "Okay, I might have to let them take you a little."

"What?"

Vrrnwaaaaauuummmm!

One of them flew over us. Flying geezer zombies?

Okay, now we were officially screwed.

"Wha... wait! What's th--"

Vrrrrnnzzzzzzznnnnnttttt!

Three geezer gimps, clumped together rocketed over my head and, incredibly, I felt their grip loosen just slightly.

Something black and slick came down on my chest for a moment, and it hurt.

Looking up, the face was just above me.

Not a gimp.

"What are you guys playin' at?"

"Old dude! What the hell is--"

Grrnzzzznntttttt!!

The black thing bit into me slightly then flew up, taking another handful of rotting, drooling zombies with it.

As it passed over me, I saw another one-- they were wheels.

Craning my neck back, the old sunofagun stripped the zombie corpses off of the front of his electric scooter, his Rascal, which he'd mounted and tied off three busted rake handles to its wired shopping basket.

It's huge tires spun, spitting zombie flesh behind it--

"Move out the way!"

-- he drove the scooter right between Chubbs and me and I heard the sounds of cracking bone, tearing of flesh.

"Gotcha, bastards!"

Chubbs cried out, "I'm loose, man! General, you okay? Wher--"

Struggling, twisting, still I couldn't break free.

Almost, almost-- then one of them wrapped me by the wrist and yanked at me.

"Hey, kid,"-- it wasn't one of the gimps. The old guy put my hand at the base of the Rascal's wire basket. He smiled, wildly, "Now don't let go."

Whrrrrnnnnnnnnnnnn!

The machine whine, complained until it finally broke free, pulling my body with it with disgusting slrummptnt! sound, Chubbs cheering and waving his Octx in the air, running right behind us.

He held on, my fingers like steel, as my eyes began to fill with sunlight, we headed backwards, toward the doors.

"HOLD TIGHT!"

Crash!

The doors split open and we wheeled backwards into the front lot, with my partner coming through door (with only a brief stop to strike into a garbled mash of dead zombie flesh, "Asshole!"), and I felt, strangely, like I'd been reborn.

We weren't going to be gummed and eaten by geezer zombies. At least, not yet.

MY SECOND IN COMMAND (of two) is prone to, let's say, impulse.

This is, likely, already clear.

"Come on, man!"

"I don't know," I said again. "Seriously?"

We'd ridden the Rascal up the road to just within sight of the CDC. The old guy explained that he'd been a mechanic years back, up in Chicago, and had outfitted his Rascal with some upgrades.

The big mag wheels for example-- not standard issue.

When I'd asked him why he'd done it, why he'd tinkered with an old man scooter, he'd replied: "Kids don't visit me much anymore. So I was blowing their inheritance any way I could."

Okay. Makes sense.

He was also, he'd explained, a big fan spending that inheritance at local strip clubs. Especially those that didn't pay their "dancers" very well. "Seedy," then seemed to describe not just the types of places his visited but also it's staff.

This, I'd asked him repeated, to talking about.

"Not my fault," he said. "I know for a fact, they've been testing out boner medicine on us at the home. Not my fault if I got a little lead in my penci, again!"

"You. Must. Stop."

"So what if I guy gets randy every now and again," he said, steering the little Rascal, me and Chubbs holding onto either side of it. I looked to my partner, he didn't even seem to be listening-- just digging the wind in his hair, enjoying the ride.

"Okay, I get it--"

"There's a place called Puppets, just off Hiway 78, you know it?"

Gripping tightly on the scooter, I said, "No, and I don't want--"

"They should have called it Finger Puppets, if you know what I mean," he said, popping his eyebrows like rabid, evil caterpillars.

"I'm begging you, plea--"

"Even had an unofficial 'Knuckle-deep Night,' where for two bucks--"

"STOP, man!"

And, he did. He stopped talking and stopped the Rascal.

I'd called Chubbs over for an official Swordsmen conference.

Yes, he'd helped us out and, yes, we could use any help we could if we were goingto Save Humankind.. But the guy was so old and so, so gross!

"Let's having him be a part of our group, General," Chubbs said. "Two people, an army don't make."

In truth we needed him, it seemed. Well, we needed anyone. And, all cards on the table, it was kind of hard to say no, especially since Chubbs had begun to call me General. That was pretty cool.

My second in command saw me wavering and his big smile came back in full force. "Come on, all we gotta do is name him and he's officially in."

Still, I wasn't sure.

We walked back to the old man and his Rascal® where he waited, trying to look like he wasn't listening.

I laid it out: "Would you be interested in-- not a formal invitation now!-- but would you entertain the idea of joining us to try and save the entire human race?"

"Sure, okay."

"Wait, wait, wait-- don't get too riled up about it yet," I said. "We'll have to spend some time--"

Chubbs interrupted, "What's your name?"

The old guy eyed him. "Why?"

"You need a name to be in The Swordsman!"

"The what?"

"It's like a warrior name. But it's got to reflect our shared condition, right?"

The old guy looked at me now: "Is he okay?"

"Yeah," I said, "He gets on a roll. Go with it, best bet."

"So, I'm Chubbs, which is a nice little double entendre. And this is the General, he's the leader--"

A little bit of pride swelled in me, and I couldn't help but smile.

"and it's also short for Little General. Meaning a pee-pee, see?"

Still swelling but all traces of pride gone in an instant.

We got back onto the Rascal and all rumbled down the road toward the Centers for Disease Control. If there were anyone left there-- scientists, experts, anyone-- we had to let them know what we'd learned about the ED medicine. It could be humanity's last hope.

"Well, I'll help you out, but I don't want any of your weird club names. Too old for that."

"What should we call you, then?"

"Dammit, just call me by real name: Mr. Johnson," he said and the two of us said nothing. "Nothing fancy, I'm sorry. Just plain ol' Mr. Johnson to you two."

The whirring of the motor filled the air, as the sun began to creep slowly toward the horizon. I let my eyes flicker just a little toward Chubbs, who was grinning enjoying the ride.

He was quiet for a moment, until he couldn't hold it any longer.

"It's like destiny, man."

"NO, it's not like destiny!"

Despite that, his smile grew just a little bit larger.

OF COURSE, IF HE knew then what we know now... if he knew what we were about to discover at the CDC. That smile would have drained from his face, possibly taking all future smiles with it.

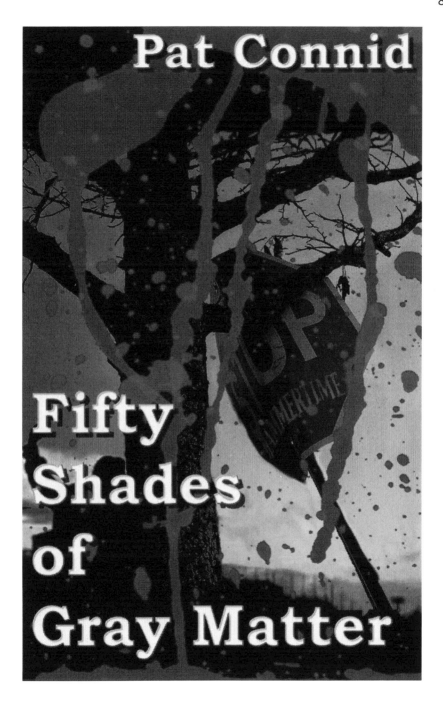

BOOK THREE

"Where do you think that goes?"

We'd taken Mr. Johnson's Rascal® around the entire CDC campus but never saw a single person. And while there were a handful of cars strewn about, it didn't seem anyone had driven these to work that particular day.

Every vehicle we'd seen had been upended and burnt crispy. And most, if not all of them, were those little lunch-box-on-roller-skates Smart Cars. So, yeah, it was sorta hard to really feel bad about it.

Systematically, we checked each and every entrance. All of them, locked.

And, I'll admit-- only now-- to not pulling very hard on any particular door, for my part.

Sure, I wanted to get inside and tell the eggheads what we'd learned-- that the same medicine guys take for a bout of "the softies," can help stave off the effects of total zombification (or Full Zombie-- FZ).

I'd learned that by accident, after trying to off myself in a CVS Pharmacy in downtown Atlanta.

My former girlfriend (she was my then- girlfriend, but that was before I had to bash her zombie skull in with her favorite piece of apartment décor: a tin frog band that had be set up on a living room shelf) had infected me with a nip on the pink parts.

I'd seen what folks went through when they'd become gimps.

Bad skin, poor vocabulary (mostly variations of mrrrnarrrhh and rrrrnnaaanzzt) and a love of two things-- human flesh and interstate driving.

This left half the population, the non-undead ones, who (in an aggressive choice to ignore the new folks at the top of the food chain) were trying to go about their daily routine, living in quiet fear of becoming a zombie smoothie before their afternoon one-on-one with the boss.

After being bitten by my girl, I hadn't wanted to end up being a part of the zombie horde, so after breaking into the drug store, I'd downed handfuls of what appeared to be pain meds.

But instead of drifting off to permanent sleep, I experienced-- what you might call-- a severe, unnatural stirring below the belt.

Turns out, they weren't pain pills. I'd found jars and jars of ED medicine. And while, sure, it got a bit uncomfortable walking around all day like that (the tip gets a wee tender, truth be told), having that little bit of blood redirected away from the brain kept me from becoming Full-Zombie (instead living as a Near-Zombie or NZ (Oh yes, we've devised a couple difficult, cumbersome designations here (re: FZ and NZ), but you'll get the hang of it in time).

A few hours after that, I'd found Chubbs just about dead and got him on the same regimen as me. Both of his hands were chewed away, down to the mid-forearm, so he'd replaced each of them with handheld stop signs that he'd found next to a couple of dead crossing guards.

Yeah, you can laugh, but his Octx (as he calls them) are deadly.

Our third member (okay, ha ha, totally unintentional, let it go) we'd found in an overrun nursing home. Mr. Johnson was in his eighties and was also Near-Zombie-- surviving the attack because he was, of all things, on an ED medicine "patch" (something he hadn't yet fully explained).

Yes, we are the ones you've heard about.

We are the turgid.

We are The Swordsman.

Our quest: to Save All of Humankind .

Because we were all that was standing between the uninfected and an army of hungry gimps.

Clearly, the odds were not in our favor.

IN THE PARKING LOT of the CDC, we plugged Mr. Johnson's tricked-out old man scooter into an outlet to charge, then walked toward a hidden ramp that'd we'd stumbled upon while surveying the complex.

"Intel, son," Mr. Johnson had said. "We need intel!"

He'd been barking that at me again, moments earlier, when he clipped a wheel stop, which sent us spinning off into a thicket of evergreen trees. From that vantage point (after getting up off our backs, of course), we'd seen the hidden, concrete ramp.

Now, I'm not an expert in the covert, but a sudden cluster of fir trees doesn't strike me as a terribly good way to hide any type of "super-secret" ramp leading into the United

States' repository for the most dangerous diseases in the world.

First, because it this was the only cluster of evergreens in sight. In fact, the only other trees we could even see were on the other side of the railroad tracks we'd crossed earlier.

So, this attempt at camouflage was the architectural equivalent of someone, let's say, not wanting to be recognized in a crowd, so they slap on one of those big, fake Hercule Poirot mustaches. No one's buying it.

And, second, making it slightly more conspicuous was that, having been there as "cover" for several years, I suppose, it appeared some office busy-body had gone to decorating them each winter with Christmas lights, boxes and boxes of tinsel and ornaments as big as a baby's head.

Eventually, putting up and taking down the decorations was likely a hassle, so it seems they simply left them up all year long-- maybe only turning on the strings of colored lights during the holiday season.

"Oh, Christ, that looks pathetic," Mr. Johnson said as he got up slowly, after being tipped out of the Rascal®. "That tinsel looks like three month old spaghetti. Ornaments look like my old roommate's balls."

"Really? I don't need that," I said. "Not imagery easy to clear out of the mind, man."

"You're kind of a nasty old dude, ain't cha?"

Chubbs was right. The most senior Swordsman was one of the dirtiest men I'd ever met.

Johnson snorted at Chubbs. "You call me nasty? This coming from a guy whose insides is dripping down a pair stop signs where his hands are supposed to be."

"Am I dripping?" Chubbs' voice lifted an octave, and he looked down quickly.

"No, don't worry about it," I said, then pointed through the trees to the concrete ramp, hidden just beyond the nightmarish Christmas trees. "Where do you think that goes?"

Mr. Johnson surprised me a little-- he walked up and slipped deeper into the trees to get a look. For a moment, he was out of sight.

Chubbs and I held back for a second-- if there were going to be a zombie sneak attack, you know, we could cover the old fellah from behind.

We "got his six," as they say. Actually, me and Chubbs were a little spread a part, not exactly behind him, so I had more his eight while Chubbs had about quarter-after four.

But, close enough.

"Well," he said coming back a minute later. "From the looks of it-- given the way the building is situated. It looks like the ramp... it goes, you know, down."

I stared for a moment but, nope, that was the intel our old scout had brought back. The ramp, it appeared, goes down.

Helpful.

Earlier, Chubbs had been all gung-ho about storming into the old folks' home-- to even the score with his father it seems-- but now he was looking a little wide-eyed at the ramp leading into the bowels of the CDC.

"We just, you know, gonna go in there? Don't they have a help-line or something we can call first?"

"Did that-- just got voicemail."

Johnson chimed in, "I bet the whole place is overrun with droolin' gimps. I'm pretty sure this was the first place that was attacked. Payback, really."

"Payback? What's that supposed to mean?"

Mr. Johnson looked between me and Chubbs. He started to talk, then stopped.

"What's what supposed to mean?"

Chubbs shook his head, and I said: "What do you mean by pay--HEYYY!"

From out of the evergreens, probably from up the ramp, a half dozen gimps lumbered toward us.

Johnson took a couple high steps away from the tree line and me and Chubbs crept, backwards, toward the old man's scooter.

"Keep an eye out for others," I said.

"Totally," Chubbs agreed. "Like Jurassic Park. They distract you and then whammo! come at you from the sides."

"Yes, yes! EXACTLY."

Johnson wasn't moving as fast as we were-- the gimps closing the gap a little-- and I told him to pick up the pace.

"Nah, these are undeadies from up at the nursing home," he said, but still kept his distance. "And they're from the ward we used to call 'death row.' Old as dirt. You don't have to outrun these ones because they haven't run since the Coolidge administration."

"How can you be sure?" Chubbs wasn't yet convinced and readied his Octx while balancing himself up on the balls of his feet: his fighting stance.

Seeing this, I warned him, "Seriously, man, don't start the singing. We're not fighting these guys, no need to sing that god-awful song."

"It helps me concentrate, get my rhythm down, man," he said with that big Chubbs' grin of his.

"I just want to go on record," I said, keeping my eyes on our geezer-gimp pursuers. "It's about even money, but I may be less afraid of being eaten alive than I am of having an MC Hammer song rolling through my head as it happens."

Johnson walked up next to us and turned back toward the small group of super-old gimps. He was right: for zombies, they were really moving slow.

"That one on the left, that's Adele Windlesmith."

"Yeah? How do you know?"

Johnson said, "Well, for one, during a Tuesday movie night I finger-banged her during Old Yeller."

"Dude!" Chubbs yelled and put his Octx up to cover his ears, inadvertently slicing off the lobe of the left one. "Ow, ow. That's all stingy, now. Damn hard to get used to these things," he said. "But, seriously, Mr. Johnson, you gotta stop with the old geezer nasty talk man... it upsets my stomach."

"Yeah, I have to second that emotion."

Johnson snorted and waved us off.

"Well, if your tender ears will permit," he went on, "the other reason I knows it's her is because of her... uh, her pillow pets."

Chubbs scrunched up his face and looked at him.

Johnson clarified: "Her funsacks, son. Her boobs."

"Seriously?"

"No, I mean it. While we were at the home, she got fake boobies," he said. "A lot of the ladies did."

The small group of gimps were within about 15 feet of us, gurgling and reaching out with crooked fingers, so we started slowly walking away from them, in a circle.

Yeah, not the biggest threat, but old folks can be sneaky-- even the undead ones.

"Is that all you guys did? You said before a lotta the old guys were on Viagra. Now, you're telling us the old grannies at the home were getting boob jobs," Chubbs said. "Gawd, I never knew old people were so nasty! Totally screws up my heads about my gammy." He shivered. "Ugh, so awful!"

The oldest Swordsman shrugged.

"There's only so much backgammon you can play," he said then was quiet for a moment, as we watched the old geezer gimps hobble toward us. He added: "You just gotta get the tip wet every now and then."

"Dude!"

"Okay, okay," Mr. Johnson said. "That one just slipped out."

For the next few minutes, as the early afternoon sun beat down upon us, The Swordsman-- three who would Try to Help Save the World with ED Medicine-- we just walked in a big circle while the super old gimps followed us, snarling, gurgling, occasionally swiping.

I had to consider our next move. Certainly, there were concerns about busting into the CDC guns-a-blazing.

For one-- we didn't know what to expect. And if we did find the viral scientists working on the ZBF, would they see us as help or-- given our condition (the Near-Zombie thing, not the permanent erections thing)-- would we been seen as saviors... or the enemy?

For two, to actually "go in guns a-blazing," one usually needs, you know, guns.

This was exactly the point Mr. Johnson had been going on about when I turned around to see Chubbs toying with the geezer zombies.

"... and I don't care much if most of my body is raging with zombie spice making me nearly immune to killin'--"

I frowned and said to Johnson, "Zombie spice?"

"-- I'm a veteran," he said, ignoring me. "And when you fight in a war, and we are in a war, make no mistake, you need armament, son. Bigger the better."

He told me about a surplus store up the road, a guy he knew. We agreed that before we'd make a run at getting inside the complex, there'd be a quick pit stop at the surplus place to see if we could pick up some stuff that went "boom."

As I mulled this over, watching Chubbs mess with the old gimps a bit, suddenly something the old guy said sounded off.

"Hold on, what war were you in?"

"Back in '69," he said. "I still have dreams about it. Horrible."

Chubbs used his teeth to pull out half of a fruit roll up from his shirt pocket. He carefully unfurled it, using his Octx.

As I stood there a little impressed that he was getting the hang of his new hands, I watched as he took the compressed sheet of fruit and sugar, carried it between his Octx and, unnoticed at first, placed it on the back of one of the geezer zombies.

When he jumped away, two of the other undeadies caught the sickly-sweet scent of it and attacked the fruit roll up zombie.

"Chubbs, don't do that," I said, then turned back to Johnson. "Uh, I don't mean to be rude but you look a little... old to have been in Vietnam. You would have been in your forties or?--"

"Forty wasn't too old for 'Nam, son."

My stomach sank, and I really felt like a jerk. Here was this war vet and--

"But, I wasn't in Vietnam."

Chubbs was grinning huge, even giggling, as he watched the two gimps do a slow-tackle of the Fruit Rollup Zombie, all three of them going to the ground with the two on top, biting and snapping at the red fruit semi-circle on the one on the bottom.

"What other-- 1969?-- where, then? An American war?"

Johnson stiffened up and said, "Yes, an American war!"

"I'm sorry, I don't--"

"Middle America."

"Middle? You mean like... Iowa?"

"No, no, no," he said and spit on the concrete as he watched Chubbs toying with the gimps. "Central. Central America. I was seeing a young filly who lived in Honduras. Town called Oco-tuh-picky or some damn thing."

With the gimps no longer, remotely, a concern-- they were now sort of doing slow crawls over top of each other trying to get the roll-up-- I leaned against the back of Rascal® and Johnson took his spot up in the driver's seat.

If we were going to head out, we'd have to do it soon. Daylight was fading.

"Wow, I never heard about that? Some secret American war, then?"

"Well, no not really. Not U.S. 'American' that is. Just a couple of little countries all fighting over some soccer match."

My head was spinning-- either from the story or I'd have to dose again soon (to keep the zombie within at bay).

"It... what? Soccer? Whose side were you on then?"

"Neither," he said and began fiddling with the wooden stakes he'd tied to the wire basket. "I'd been at their soccer stadium under the bleachers, had the girl down to her skivvies, when all hell broke loose. Bombs going off, jeeps tied to planes shooting down at us..." He drifted off for a moment. "I was so close to hitting pay dirt, too. God, she was a beauty."

Shaking my head, I stood and walked toward Chubbs, then turned back.

"Listen, if you're part of The Swordsman, and if we're very likely going into some sort of firefight down in the basement of that complex... I need to know if you're bat-shit crazy or not, man!"

He stared at me for a moment and then leaned across the scooter's handle bars.

"Depends on what you mean by that. How do you figure bat-shit crazy?" He scratched his chin. "Do you mean crazy like three guys, all a heart-beat away from becoming flesh-eating monsters... one in his eighties, another with two railroad spikes sticking out of his chest, and the last with stop signs where his hands should be... three guys, by the way who want to save mankind by fighting off a zombie apocalypse in a Rascal® scooter with a backpack of ED medicine armed with only, at this point in time, three purple-tipped baby-makers?" He stood up, and put his hands on his little, bony hips and his fingers curled down as if parenthesis to what he'd just said. "You mean that kind of bat-shit crazy?"

I raised my arms, tilted my head, and said: "It was a simple question. You don't have to get all showy."

"Hey, Hal!"

Nodding, I pointed a thumb toward Chubbs. Johnson just waved me off and went back to tightening the busted-rake-handles-cum-wooden-spears that he'd bound to the front of his scooter.

"We... Chubbs, seriously?"

When I'd come up, the geezer gimps each had a limb of another in their mouths, chewing away but not finding anything really good, moving along an inch or so, and trying another spot.

The fruit roll up had fallen off and a twisted up in some dirt about three feet away from the six writhing zombies.

Watching his "show," Chubbs walked over, flipped the roll-up up with an Octx, and began to eat it slowly.

"Oh my god, dude, that's nasty."

"You know," he said as he chewed, "the two ladies here, they're the meanest ones. The dude gimps are just dumb, but the gimp grannies--"

I sighed and said, "Let's go man."

"--they're mean suckers. And Mr. Johnson was right. They're undead grannies but they both got some nice knockers."

"Okay, that's all kinda blechy man, let's go."

Chubbs walked past the gimps, and they hardly noticed him. He stopped, then said--

"Wait a sec. We don't even know, you know, really anything about these things."

Starting to walk toward the Rascal®, I stopped, and turned back. Chubbs had something on his mind. And, in truth, I really didn't want to know what it was. But, we had to get moving.

"Yeah? And?"

"Well," he said. "You know, if we, like, cut off the head, does that kill them or do you gotta get at the brain?"

"I, uh, it doesn't so much--"

"See?" He knelt down next to the undeadies-- only the women had teeth, not likely their own, so the guys were just zombie gumming at the others. "What if a lotta these things are coming at us, right? We gotta know what makes them dead instead of undead."

"You just, I mean..."

Mr. Johnson whirred up on his Rascal®, startling me.

"What is it about you old people?" I said, jumping back. "Always creeping around, sneaking up on people!"

"You know, Chubby's got a point," Johnson said. "General, we have almost zero intel on those creatures."

"Stop saying 'intel.' Can you do me that favor?"

"Hal," Chubbs said, put his foot out, and pinned the ropy neck of one of them with his shoe-- it didn't seem to notice. "We don't even know if lopping the head off is enough to kill these things."

I was already worried about the sun going down and us having to make our way back from Johnson's arms dealer friend then navigating the CDC complex in the dark. So leaving a.s.a.p., that was my first priority, and I told them that.

They both turned quiet for a moment.

"Well, you're the leader of this outfit," Mr. Johnson finally said. "And, I know in war-time, you have got to have faith in your leader."

"You were in a war??"

I glanced over at Chubbs and gave him my Seriously, don't even go there look.

Chubbs said, "What war?"

Obviously, I needed to work on my communicative expressions a bit.

"Let's not get into that again," I said, took a deep breath and looked to the sky for some sort of inspiration.

With the soothing backdrop of softy, pillowy clouds, a beautiful songbird swooped and flitted through the air, coasting along on the updrafts.

Peaceful.

It used to be like that down here, too. Well, not entirely peaceful, but we didn't used to have an undead army trying to eat the rest of us.

Only a day earlier, I'd had a girlfriend that I'd cared about, even loved.

And, who knows, we may have even gotten married one day. She was as close as I'd ever been to another person. And I think she felt the same way.

In fact, I remember the very day I'd felt that from her.

It was just a casual afternoon, just talking, and while she was saying something about whatever she was going on about, she went into the bathroom, sat down and just kept talking.

Startling at first, but not because she was making soft thwop noises-- it struck me that we'd gotten to the point, a rare relationship crossroads, where we felt comfortable enough to use the toilet in front each other.

Door wide open, faded undies stretched out lazily between two cute, knobby knees... that day, as I stood there many months earlier, my eyes had begun to water.

I was moved emotionally, sure, but she also was just tearin' up that bathroom. Wuff.

But, all this time later, as I plotted with my fellow Swordsmen , facing impossible odds... for a moment, I teared up once again.

Because, at least one time, I'd earned a good woman's love.

Or indifference.

Either way-- ultimately, it was at least just nice to not have to close the bathroom door.

I glanced back up to the sky, briefly, to see the bird one last time. And as I began to look away, another larger bird, with huge talons, swept down, gripped the thing and ate it-- midair-- head first.

I turned to Chubbs: "What'd you have in mind?"

"ALAS, POOR YORICK," CHUBBS said, with a surprisingly impressive British accent. "I knew him, Horatio, a fellow of infinite jest, of most excellent fancy."

The geezer gimp's head-- no body anymore-- was balanced on the flat of one of Chubbs' stop signs. As he held it aloft, the head said:

"Bllnaaaarrrnnnn!"

Mr. Johnson banged his hands together softly, applauding.

"You're quite good. Missed your calling, boy"

"That wasn't what I had in mind, man," I said walking over to Chubbs and the decapitated head. First, we'd fed it a couple ED tablets, but it must have been too far gone. No effect.

So, Chubbs had lopped off its head.

"No body, but it's still alive, though, huh?"

"Yeah, don't get it."

Chubbs leaned in a little toward the head and it hissed at him, phlegm splattering his Octx. My friend frowned and bopped the gimp head with his other sign.

Blam!

"Oh hey, that made a blam noise!" I said, then added: "But, seriously, don't do that. It's not helping."

"Pffft! He's dead, man. Whatever."

"No, not dead," I said, balancing the creature's head back onto the sign so it didn't fall off. "It's undead and this poor thing didn't do a dam-- mutherofcatnipples- whattheff--!"

As I'd steadied it, the geezer gimp had gotten my thumb in its mouth and was gnawing at the tip until Chubbs bopped it again.

Blam!

Its eyes rolled for a moment and it let go, then growled at me.

I looked down at my hand-- it had bitten off the tip of my thumb!

When I looked back at the creature, it actually looked like it was smiling.

Chewing and smiling.

"OKAY!" CHUBBS CALLED OUT as he put the last of empty tall-boy beer can in place, but I'd already chucked it and he had to high step out of the way as the zombie head went nose-ear-nose-ear-nose-ear rolling toward the stack of cans.

Clank, clink, clink!

"Yay!" They both cheered me as I knocked down almost all the cans with the gimp's noggin.

"Aw, damn," I said. "Left one standing."

Under a small pile of cans, about thirty feet away, we heard:

"Blllrrarranntt!"

"You didn't give it enough English," Johnson said as we walked toward the cans.

"Was that it? I'm not-- I've really never bowled."

"Oh, it's great for the kids."

A minute later, cans restacked-- CLANK, clink, clink, clink, thunk!

"Yes!"

"Wow, you were right, just gotta throw a little spin into it."

"Mnnnaarrrptttttt!"

"NO, NO, YOU CAN'T push it, that's totally cheating!"

"Rules," Mr. Johnson said, holding the arms of his gimp to steer it from behind. "There ain't no rules."

Chubbs had Johnson dig into his pocket and the old guy had come out with a handful of chocolate Raisenettes. He then proceeded to slice two of the geezer gimps in half with a couple clean swipes of his Octx, and with Johnson's help (and insistence), they propped up the two gimps facing each other... and proceeded to stuff the Raisenettes up the nostrils of both zombies.

Then, as the drooling undeadies began to notice how tasty the other looked-- they seemed to still love candy-- Chubbs and Johnson each got behind one, and tried steering them-- whichever one got the chocolate raisins outta the other gimp first would be the winner.

"I wish I had a camera," I said watching the contest. "Oh, yeah I do!"

My phone had gotten a bit banged up in my pocket during our run-in with the old folks' home zombies-- but still a quarter charge.

I held it up and tried to get them all in the shot.

"Got it!"

Looking down at the image, I smiled.

See? There was still a little joy left in the world.

In the corner of the little screen, I caught a glimpse of the time. It really was getting late.

"You wanna give it a try, Hal?" Chubbs said, as he did his best to work his undeady toward the other. Johnson leaned his in and it gnashed its teeth, inches away from a win!

"No, man," I said, looking at the time on my phone again. "We gotta go."

"Aw, this awesome!" Chubbs said, "It's like 'Rock'em Sock'em Robots,' zombie-style!"

"'Hungry, Hungry Hippos' more like it," Mr. Johnson said.

I shrugged, "Me-- from over here-- I'm actually leaning toward the Robot game."

IT WASN'T LONG AFTER that we were on our way toward an Army surplus store that Johnson had been in from time to time. The owner had been in a real war-- Korea.

Or maybe that was a "conflict"...

Either way, the guy had served in the U.S. military and had been in combat. He now ran a surplus store a few blocks from the nearby high school.

Chubbs and I held on as Mr. Johnson steered his Rascal® through the mostly empty streets. Every now and then we'd come across a car, puttering along, a gimp inside, banging away at the steering wheel, and we'd whizz around it, pretty much unnoticed.

Chubbs yelled over the wind whipping by: "How fast are we going?"

"This thing don't have no speedometer, now. But we're probably going about twenty-five or thirty miles an hour."

Gripping it a bit tighter, I asked him, "How did you get this little thing to go that fast?"

"Told ya," Johnson shrugged, eyes glued to the road. "I was a mechanic for years. In fact, the new electric motor I put in this, I got from Charlie. Charlie is the guy who runs the surplus store."

I yelled over the wind: "What sort of guns does this guy sell?"

Johnson banked a little to the left; he'd seen a gimp on the opposite side of the road, walking in the other direction.

This thing looked like, at one time, it'd been some teenager, given that its pants were all bagged up, drooping just below the beltline.

The creature was snarling, bloodied, clawing at the air-- it didn't even see as us we came up behind. Johnson leaned a little more to the left, and Chubbs split the head in half with one slice of his left Octx.

"Clean kill, Chubby."

"Thank you, Mr. Johnson."

Every now and then, like that moment, it felt like I was floating outside my body and looking down. And, over the past twenty-four hours it was hard not to argue that the entire world had gone crazy.

"HEY, it's a zombie Ronald McDonald!"

Totally, bat-shit, unadulterated, one hundred percent no-money-back-guarantee crazy.

The sun was creeping real close to the horizon, and we hadn't even gotten to the surplus store.

"Yeah, leave it--"

"You know," Johnson said matter-of-factly, "There was one of them Ronald Houses around here but it got overrun. Guy probably worked there."

Chubbs was staring at the burger clown-- really, really staring.

"It's getting late, man, let's keep--"

And, he jumped.

"Hey, man, what are you..?"

He rolled a couple times, his metal signs banging against the blacktop like a rattling, metallic klaxon. In one quick move, he was back up on his feet. Johnson wheeled the scooter in a U-turn, but kept watch on our man.

"Impressive," he muttered.

"Used to be a rodeo protection athlete," I said. "Until the work dried up."

"Ain't much sadder than a clown without no rodeo."

I nodded, thought about that for a moment, then asked: "Very deep-- you just make that up?"

"What? No," he said. "I mean, yes. What? What are you talking about..."

"Nothing, nothing." Forgive me for settling into a philosophical mood as mankind comes to an end.

"I'm just saying 'rodeo clown, no rodeo'... that is a sad, sad thought."

We slowed as we got a bit closer to Chubbs closing in on gimp Ronald-- it stumbled along slurping, arms waving, hands balled up into fists.

Ain't much sadder than a clown without no rodeo.

It occurred to me that I hadn't the first clue of what had set Chubbs off, but my first thought was he was going to do some serious, serious ninja/ginsu-knife thing with ol' Ronald and I'd had my fill of really disturbing images I'll never squeegee clear of my mind's eye.

"Chubbs, man, leave it be," I said half-heartedly. But, this seemed like something personal.

Who was I to take it away from him?

This might be the last day he or I ever get on this planet. And a man's gotta do what a man's gotta do. Even if it's a former rodeo clown disemboweling a former burger clown.

"Well, that's a bummer," I heard Johnson say as he rolled the scooter to a stop. "Thought he was going to... what is he doing?"

From about fifty feet away, we watched as Chubbs walked up to zombie Ronald. He then banged his signs together and got its attention.

The creature spun, saw Chubbs and came at him fast.

Terrifying in its hunger, it almost had forgotten how to run properly, trading quick steps for short jumps... blood and spittle flinging from its mouth as it raced toward our friend.

But Chubbs just waited for it. Almost serenely.

We could hear the horrible, phlegmy roar rattle in its windpipe, through a mouth of broken teeth and gore.

It got closer-- Chubbs didn't move.

Then, he put his Octx down at his sides.

"Chubbs," I said quietly. "What are you doing man?"

It came at him-- faster and faster, twisting into a frenzy as it breathed the smell of the man standing right there-- his flesh, his blood, so close now!

It felt like my heart had stopped.

Ain't much sadder than a clown without no rodeo.

Oh my god, what was he doing?

The snarling creature just ten feet from him, he hadn't lifted his Octx yet. They were just there, crossed in front of his chest.

"What in the hell is that boy doin'?"

I yelled out: "Chubbs!"

Then, the creature lunged for him and, in a quick move, Chubbs slid to his right, holding his left sign-- his bright red sign-- in place as the gimp closed in.

"Oh, hell, just like a bull-- the dumb ass thing is going for the color red!"

We could hear his shoes grind stones and grit in the road as he spun-- the zombie leaping at the red sign-- Chubbs then raising his right Octx and coming down onto the thing's skull, splitting the back from its front.

Zombie Ronald stopped, dead in its tracks, stunned.

For a moment, it wobbled slightly, then turned only its head to look at the man standing next to him.

Chubbs pulled his Octx back out, bloodied, and a moment later, the gimp clown's head split into two like a banana peel, and it dropped to its knees, then to the ground.

Johnson got the scooter moving again and headed to pick up our friend.

"Hellfire, I'm glad that boy's on our side, I'll tell you that."

I said nothing, just watching as Chubbs bent down and seemed to say something to the dead creature. Then he slowly lifted a bag off its shoulder-- I hadn't noticed that before-- hooking it with his metal "hand" and slowly walked toward us.

He didn't say much as he hopped up onto the Rascal® and looped an arm around the seat to hold on. Johnson gave him a long look.

"I'm good," Chubbs said and smiled. "Let's go."

IF PATRIOTISM WERE MEASURED by the size of one's flag, then Charlie Delbert Saylor may just be the most loyal American on the planet (well, and if flag size were really a measure of Americanism, our presidents would then likely hold their inauguration ceremonies at Perkins restaurants).

The problem, if you could call it that, was that Charlie never took the flag down. Ever.

So, naturally, the thing got a bit tattered.

When it did, over the years, he'd climb up a ladder with a chunk of fabric he felt matched just fine, and patch the spots that had been damaged by sun, bad weather or the annual Army Surplus Depot's Independence Day Fireworks and Beer Garden Extravaganza.

So, over 28 years in the same spot, most of the parts of his flag had been traded out, some more than once.

Now, I'd never tell him this because he's very proud of his big flag and what it stands for, but the damn thing was a mess. Mismatched colors, different fabrics... and the last time I saw stitching like that, it was on a real big fellah with a touch-and-go temper and bolts on either side of his neck.

Compared to Charlie's huge patchwork American flag, the Aids Quilt looks like some pristine Egyptian cotton, 1500-count bed sheet you might pick up at a JC Penny's white sale.

"Johnson!" Charlie was a big guy with a big smile that liked to shake hands in the same way junk yards like to crush cars. His eyes were shaded slightly by a Built Tough ball cap. "Who are your, uh, friends here?"

His shop-- we were standing at the front-- looked a little like someone had opened up their garage. Shelves upon shelves of jackets, helmets, canteens, shovels that fold up, almost everything you'd need if you were heading into battle in, say, 1951.

But for what the store couldn't boast in width, he could be proud of its length (yes, you can do your own jokes here, I'll wait...).

In a nutshell, compared to the Army Surplus Depot that long warehouse at the end of Raiders of the Lost Ark was like opening a flap on an advent calendar.

The place just goes and goes and goes.

If it was green, made out of canvass and could last for a hundred years, it was on his shelf somewhere.

As I admired his store, Charlie had rounded the counter to give his old buddy a shake of the hand. He'd seen something a little strange on ol' Johnsons' face, I'm sure: yellowed eyes, pupil's the size of pinheads. Skin gray (or grayer in Mr. Johnson's case).

Obviously, he did not know yet that his old buddy was just a few milliliters of red platelets away from being a full-on member of the Undead society.

Shaking my hand, he eyeballed me and his fears, I'll say, were not allayed.

When he'd move on to shake Chubbs' hands-- which he no longer had -- Charlie was ready, I think, to close up shop for the day and head home to get good and drunk.

"Hey Charlie," Mr. Johnson said, putting on the brave face. "How ya been, my friend?"

Charlie took a couple steps back.

"Hey, Johnson." Quick flash of a smile. "You guys trick-or-treatin' or something? What's all this about?"

The third Swordsman put an arm around his buddy's shoulder and walked him a few feet deeper into the store to tell him the story. My best guess, there were going to be a couple whopper lies in there (especially ones that made him look really good), so he didn't want to weave his heroic yarn in from of me and Chubbs.

So, the two of us waited patiently at the front of the store.

As we did, Chubbs walked over to the counter and began to dump something out. I hadn't noticed until then that he'd brought zombie Ronald McDonald's bag in with him.

I caught him, once or twice, looking sideways at me. Finally, he spoke up-- surprisingly quiet for a guy like him.

"Hey, you mind helping me with this," he said. "My hands, you know. Good for killing gimps. Not so good for just about everything else." He looked down at them for a moment. "Maybe traffic stops."

I laughed at his joke, nodded, and went over to help him separate the stuff out of the bag.

There were some random personal things in there, but what Chubbs was after- - why he'd rolled out of the scooter in the first place-- were a couple thick glass jars and, what looked like, a half-dozen grease pencils.

"I recognized the type of bag, the compartments, because I used to have one," he said, a little distant. "Back when I was with the riders and the broncs. Can you..?"

He nodded to one jar and I turned its lid a couple times until it came open. Inside it looked like just white paste. But it wasn't paste.

I said, "Clown make up."

Smiling, he shrugged.

"It's what I'm good at, right?" He then added: "I never wanted to be a damn rodeo protect-- rodeo clown. Not at all. Hated it a lot of the time," he said. He leaned back against the counter, looked down at his Octx, then back at me, blinking away some dampness.

"I know, man," I said. "I saw you beat your undead daddy to death over it."

"Yeah, but I'm okay about it now."

Which was a nice little epiphany for Chubbs, but the timing hadn't really work out for his old man. Ah, such is life. Family! Right?

"I'm… this is who I am, General," he said, then grinned one of his great Chubbs smiles. "Hal." He laughed. "I'm a gimp-slaying rodeo clown. And… I'm good at."

"Okay," I said and put my hand on his shoulder. "I'll support you any way I can."

"Great," he looked back at me, relieved. "Can you put some of this make up on me?"

I looked down at the jars, then back at my friend.

"Is there any other way that I can support you?"

"OKAY FELLAHS, LET'S GET some gear," Mr. Johnson said as he walked up. "I let Charlie in on some of our plan and... what in the hell are you doin'?"

As they walked up, Chubbs was facing me with his eyes closed, head held steady, while I gingerly dabbed black face makeup around his eyes.

"I'm... uh, well--"

Chubbs said, "Hey don't worry. The General was just putting some makeup on me, man."

Despite the assurances moments earlier that he was on board "Swordsman Plan A," this, it seemed, was a bit too much for ol' Charlie.

He stepped back a couple paces from his old friend.

"Johnson, what you got yourself into with these fellers?"

"Charlie, listen..."

His friend bristled and his voice ratcheted up a notch: "I mean, first you guys all come in here-- you with these two young guys, which is frankly a little weird you hanging with a couple of kids."

"Charl--"

"And don't think I didn't notice you all came in, uh, a little bit riled up, if you know what I mean." He looked over at Johnson and then looked down at me.

Sure, we needed the guy's help... but I don't care who you are-- I don't like my junk to be ogled at by anybody.

"Hey, crazy army dude," I said, scowling, then snapped my fingers up by my face. "Eyes up here. Rude!"

"Now," he said through gritted teeth, turning it up another notch, "I don't know what--"

"Listen up!" I finally barked at him, taking an aggressive step forward (then, actually, turned around and put down the vial of eye make-up I'd been holding-- then did my aggressive step move again). "The three of us may be all this world's got standing between you and those blood-gargling, free-range gimps that are crawling the streets hell bent on making you something they eventually squeeze out of their gray, veiny butt cheeks."

Mr. Johnson grimaced, "Steady on, son."

"No!," I growled and took another step forward-- this time both Johnson and Charlie inched backward. "As the world just keeps spinning like there's nothin' going on, yet getting darker by the hour, can you guess who are the only ones risking their lives to stop a zombie army that is actively hunting, first, any human not yet infected and, second, two big fucking slices of bread to put them between?!?"

The surplus store man blinked, then said, "Was that a question, Hal, because it got real long near the end, and I got lost halfw--"

"We ARE!" I yelled. "We are all you got, man!"

I spun in a half circle and threw my hands up, staring out the front bay window.

Looking out at the darkening sky, I continued: "Us! THREE guys! A post-suicidal, entry level graphic designer; a foul-mouthed senior citizen; and an ex-rodeo clown that has to worry he might slice off a nut every time he wipes his ass!"

"Hey, hey," Charlie mumbled, "Let's keep on topic here, guys."

Spinning back to Charlie, I roared: "SO CAN WE JUST GET A LITTLE FREAKIN' CO-OP-ER-ATION???"

Charlie stepped forward, out of the shadows and stood next to his old friend again. He looked at his shoes, then his hands and then Mr. Johnson.

"Johnson, I mean... I didn't intend to offend y'all," he said. "I knows you said you were going into battle, but I didn't know you meant that literally." He looked over at me, his face intense... but it was a different type of intensity than before. His eyes sparkled just a little. "You guys are really taking on these things? You're battling the monsters. For the rest of us."

Charlie slipped off his Built Tough ball cap and wrung it between his thick, dirt-stained fingers. He nodded.

"Son, I'm sorry," Charlie said, looking away. "My grandfather fought in the big war, my daddy was in the service and I was over in Laos for two years and lost a lotta good friends and half my foot." He looked briefly to Johnson. "We grumpy old fellers know all about war."

"And I appreciate that, sir."

"I just... me, I'm old in my ways and you're, well, over there putting makeup on a grown man and you're all whipping around here with stiff wiggle-sticks, it's just..." He looked over his shoulder to his friend. "I mean, you haven't gone funny on me, have ya Johnson?"

"Funny?"

"You know," he said and walked over. "Like, all nancy-boy or something."

"You think...?"

Charlie threw his hands up and said, "I don't know nuthin'. But if you've turned queer on me, man, I'd just as soon--"

"No, Charlie. Jeez!" Johnson said, then pointed to his yellowed eyes. "Look at me. Look at these guys. We're almost gimp, we are."

"What... what do you mean by that?"

Johnson walked forward, standing shoulder to shoulder next to me.

"Charlie, I didn't give you the whole picture," he said and banged Chubbs on the shoulder. "The reason we can fight these things, in part, is because we're just like them. We've all been bit-- but we got-- uh, medicine that lets us, well, keep a handle on our humanity."

Chubbs laughed. "Handle!"

"You're... you guys are zombies?"

"Just about," Johnson said. "Hal... the General here calls it 'Near-Zombie.'" He looked at me, swallowed hard, and nodded. "We're The Swordsman. There's just three of us, but we're going to fight those undead nasties until we can't no more."

Charlie took it all in and was quiet for a full minute. Then finally he said:

"You're, like, zombies... but fightin' for our side."

Mr. Johnson nodded, "Yep, you got it."

"And," Charlie added, quieter. "You ain't queer or nothin', then?"

"No," the oldest Swordsman laughed. "No, we ain't gay. Just undead, homicidal zombies."

"Alright," Charlie said and reached into his pocket, pulling out a set of keys. "Then, I'm good."

Hitting a button on the small black key chain, we heard a heavy door begin to roll open, deep in the back of the store.

"You Swordsman follow me," he said. "See if we can even up the odds a little."

We followed Charlie the Homophobe deeper into the store and ten minutes later we were on our way back to the CDC.

And, I tell you it's a bit of an understatement when I say that, after we left we had a fair amount of shit than went "boom."

STANDING AT THE LIP of the ramp, I could tell my fellow Swordsmen were on edge.

When I'd headed out the night before, this was my destination. And now that it was right there in front of me, there was... a hesitation.

Partly because this seemed like the end of a journey.

And partly because I didn't want to go in there and it find it to be all "ahh!" snarl, snap, "yaaarrhh!" gnosh, gnosh, burp!

It was dusk. We were minutes away from losing all light. My Near-Zombie super-senses seemed to max out, but I was still left with heightened strength, better hearing and-- I could have done without this one, sure-- a sense of smell so powerful, I could smell a cat's bad breath from a mile away.

And, taking a moment to reflect on that last bit, there must have been a lot of cats in this neighborhood. Blechy.

Chubbs banged his Octx together and began humming his horrible MC Hammer tune, getting his head into the game. He shifted his weight, rhythmically, from foot to foot.

"Let's do this, General."

Mr. Johnson added, "Time to kick gimp booty!"

I let out a sigh and said, "Mr. Johnson... you really think you need all of that?"

His buddy at the surplus store had shown us his secret stash. He wasn't licensed to sell guns and rifles. And the other stuff he had, I'm not sure there were licenses for a lot of it.

Chubbs had taken his role as a Swordsman a little more, well, spiritually than me and Johnson did.

His song was like a mantra. And, he didn't want any of the surplus guy's stuff. He had weapons: his Octx. They were a part of him, he said that's all he needed (and, given that he no longer had opposable thumbs, most of the other stuff was out of the question anyhow).

I had my railroad spikes for close combat, but the knapsack of ED medicine strapped to my back now shared the space with a handful of HE grenades. And if things got dicey, I had a little something extra on a long sling around my neck. Just in case.

Mr. Johnson was entirely a different story.

"Do you think you really need all of that?"

If you put Rambo, Scarface, and Dirty Harry in a room together, who would win?

None of them.

Because, Mr. Johnson had all their shit.

Three different types of riles were slung across his back, an MP5 machine gun hung from his chest (underneath which were Mexican bandito-style strips of bullets crisscrossing his chest). He had three holsters, each carrying a set of handguns.

Knives strapped to his legs, boots with spikes sticking from their toes and flash bombs on a string around his shoulders like some warlord child's candy necklace.

This put the 110-pound Mr. Johnson into a forward hunch. He looked like he was only one good sneeze away from snapping in two.

I asked him, "Why the goggles?"

He shrugged (well, he tried). "Why not?"

"Fair enough."

Chubbs had heard them like I did-- out in the parking lot, gimps that had picked up our scent were gathering, searching for us. If we didn't get inside, soon enough, they'd come this way and we'd be cornered.

"Swordsmen? Are you ready?"

My two subordinates were quiet for a moment and, since time was short, I added: "Don't worry, it's really a rhetorical question thing. Let's move, men."

The moment we began to head down the concrete ramp, I felt the temperature change, quickly cooling.

Chubbs was humming louder, his elbows pulsing in and out as he kept his Octx moving. He flashed me one of his grins-- brilliant white teeth, surrounded by the slap-dash rodeo clown makeup I'd painted him up with-- swaths of black, blood-red and off-white.

I had to agree with what Mr. Johnson had said earlier: Glad he's on our side.

Speaking of whom, the old guy was surprisingly soldier-like (for a fake war vet), sort of leading the charge, as if he was storming Normandy Bea--

"Johnson," I called out in a hoarse whisper, "Love the enthusiasm, but slow down, man."

He kept charging, huffing and puffing as he did, getting ahead of us.

"Mr. Johnson, stay with the group here!"

He chuffed, then coughed and finally said: "Can't... can't seem to stop."

Oh shit.

The weight of all those guns, grenades, bullets, knives and whatever else he was packing was pulling him down the ramp. And he was running faster.

And faster.

"Man, slow down!" I half-yelled, and heard a couple gimps in the parking lot above us respond to my voice. No way they could have missed it.

"Can't," was all he could get out, his flat feet slapped along the ramp's pavement fop-fop-fop-fop as he simply tried to steady himself.

In about twenty-five feet he'd stop, no question. In the middle of the long concrete wall was a metal door, that's where we were headed.

But, at this pace, the old fellah was going to get to the door first-- probably headfirst.

And loaded up as he was, he was going to make for a very pretty, very huge incendiary explosion.

Unbelievable.

We were about to finally reach the "Gates of Mordor" but get blown to bits as we rang the damn bell.

"Grab a hold of me, General!"

Trust me, I was trying-- but in the darkness, I didn't know what I'd be grabbing. My luck, it'd be a grenade as I separated it from its pin.

Ten feet from the door, he was nearly in a full sprint, looking like a windup toy soldier that had busted all its springs... arms banging up and down, the machine gun battering his face (thank god for the goggles, I suppose), his grenade necklace spinning around his neck like a hula-hoop.

Behind me, I heard Chubbs and he was pumping his arms as fast as he could, but no way he'd close the gap in time.

It was too late.

There was no way I was going to be able to stop him.

I PUT MY HANDS up to my face seconds before he was about to hit.

Sure, this wouldn't be enough to prevent being incinerated from the blast, but at least I didn't have to see the old guy explode... arms, limbs and bits of Mr. Johnson flying at me in the second before I was vaporized.

That wasn't the last thing I wanted to see on this Earth.

And, that, actually wasn't what happened anyhow.

With Chubbs coming up beside me, running full out, in that last second, he splayed out, holding his Octx in front of us-- both of them-- to shield me.

But, the boom... it never came.

Chubbs rolled a couple times on the ground then was back up to his feet. He bounced hard off the concrete wall, then in a quick move, he got back into his killa clown stance (but thankfully hadn't started with the singing again).

Then I noticed it--

The door was open.

And ahead in the darkness, I could hear Mr. Johnson fop-fop-fop down the hall, his steps ringing off the concrete walls inside the CDC.

Stopping, I checked on Chubbs who nodded at me that he was just fine.

When she stepped up into the doorway, I could barely make out her eyes, but it was clear she was infected with the Zombie Bird Flu.

But, she didn't really move like a gimp.

And, as impossible as it seemed... she must have opened the door in time to let Mr. Johnson through.

More importantly, she'd stopped him from becoming a human fireball (taking us with him).

With the turn of a door handle, she had saved all of our lives.

Taking a half-step over the threshold, I saw her clear enough to realize that she'd now leveled a rifle to her shoulder and, before I could say a word, she fired right at me.

"Mrrnarprttt"--plupt!

Spinning around, I finally saw it, just as the creature crumpled to the ground. It was inches away from grabbing me.

Didn't even know her name, and she'd saved my life twice before saying a word.

"You guys trying to get us all killed with all that racket?"

Chubbs looked at me and started humming his song, which got a pair of raised eyebrows from the young woman.

Behind me, another two of gimps were snarling, making their way down the ramp.

"Hey, did you see an old guy com--?"

"No time to chat," she said, waving us in. Chubbs looked toward me and I nodded.

I said, "Thanks for saving us. Really, that was incr--"

"You can return the favor," she said as she moved back into the darkness. I barely got a look at her. Short dark hair, dark skin.

And, what had been on her shirt? It looked like... no, that couldn't be right.

"Anytime," I said as I headed inside, following Chubbs.

Closing the door, we were enveloped in darkness as she slid the latch closed once again.

Inside, the cool dampness nipped at my skin.

"How about right now? Most of my girls are pinned down on the other side of the complex." She said, snapping her rifle to a leather strap on her back. "We thought we had a bead on the First Patron but got ambushed instead."

I asked: "Your girls?"

"Pinned down?" Chubbs asked before she could answer my question. "Ambushed by who?"

She started running down the hall, following the path that Mr. Johnson had taken.

She said over her shoulder, "Who do you think?"

We followed her, looking between each other. She saw us, slowed down and spun around, walking backwards as she talked:

"Are you joking? The WWF, of course."

Every answer she seemed to give us led to a dozen more questions. I could barely follow--

"You don't know," she said. Her mouth hung open for a moment. "Do you?"

We shook our heads and she continued: "I'll explain on the way and, hey, you better dose, man. I don't want you crossing over and becoming one of those things right next to me."

"What?" Had she been talking to me? How did she even know about that? I muttered, "Uh, I did, actually. About twenty minutes ago."

She gave me a long stare, then said: "Oh. How sad."

Oh damn. I said, "Hey now, no need to be--"

"NO time!" She shouted. "We have to help the ladies out, let's go!"

She raced off ahead of us, and we both chased after her.

Chubbs said-- running next to me, huffing, and sucking his breaths in hard-- "Ladies??"

BOOK FOUR

The General hadn't knowed some of young Karla's history, so it seemed right that I take a whack at her. Not at her and that hot little body of hers, ha, no!

I'm in my eighties and been around the track a fair couple times, so me, I could probably show her a few things that she'd only read about in storybooks (probably ones that got banned, too!).

But, nah, she and me, we never got to-gether together.

Now, that said, I can tell it crossed her mind, though. Sure, she let on that her affections lay elsewhere, but I knowed she was eye-balling me. Eye-ballin' and dreaming about real balling with yours truly, hah har!

Mr. Johnson suddenly stood up and quietly walked into the night.

"What! Oh, hell no, get out of here," he said, waving away at the heavens toward some unseen force. "Un-wanted, more like! I don't need no goddamn narrator! I was doing just--"

Despite his objections, he knew this story was best told by another. Actually ANYONE but him. And, as he walked away--

"I'm not goin' nowhere you stupid, unbodied, ghost voice! Ya sound like you oughta be doin' the Blue Light Special announcements at the K-Mart!"

"AS HE walked away--"

"Ain't walkin' nowhere! You can kiss my skinny, white-- !!"

As he... held his place, his feet planted firmly in the soft dirt and sand--

"Now you're hearing me. That's right!"

He felt an odd sensation at the base of his right leg, as some type of creature-- long, cold and damp-- began to slither up his calf.

"What..?"

On the left side of his body--

"Listen, come on now, let's not get--"

--a tugging, tingling around his upper, inner thigh-- and then, out of the blue-- his left testicle shrank to the size of a corn nut.

"Fwwwwoooonnnn...pffftttt!"
He said.

But it was the right side of his body that was--

"Ya made your poi--!"

-- his right side, he felt the black adder snake crawl up, slink past the curve of his knee, up his thigh--

"Now, hold on, y-you, that's my personal me-space goin' there!"

-- seeking a dark, dark cave. Something warm and slightly... moist--

"OKAY, OKAY, Jesus-H-Christ-on-a-popsicle-stick, man! Fine, your story, YOUR STORY!"

The snake continued, inches away--

"Seriously, oh man oh man, I was out of line-- where was I going? Out into the darkness, somewhere? Here I go. Story's all yours."

Johnson moved from the warm, soft light and stepped deeper into the woods.

"I'm stepping deeper into the woods."

And a moment later was out of sight.

"Yeah and up yours, too, you twisted nattering dilhole!"

That's when the snake picked up his scent again, sprang into action and made a beeline for the old man in the woods.

"Wooooaaahhhhh! Hey, fwoonnn!... leav-- wuup, wutt, wu... leaving now."

KARLA HAD BEEN BORN Karlattanita Mausoulte Dah'Inarjdad in a small village some two hundred fifty miles west-south-west of Kandahar, Afghanistan.

She'd grown up in her father's store, which, since it was perched, as it was, so close to the Iranian border, stocked and sold highly-flammable American flags to post-Friday prayer worshipers from both her home and neighboring countries as they headed to early afternoon protests.

Young Karlattanita spent most of the time in the front of the store because the back of the store... back there, she'd been frightened by what lurked there.

Before her sixth birthday, though, her mother had taken the young girl away from that place. And, at first, the young girl both loved and hated her for it. Happy to be safely away from the terrors of the back store room, but hateful, too: she'd been snatched from the only world ever known to her.

Karlattanita's mother had been regarded-- back where the winds of Sistan could blow out the sun-- for being the jewel in the crown that was Halibb's Anti-American Depot & Western Union Annex. A favorite of the disenfranchised and the young ne'er-do-well looking for a few hours to kill at a start-up, violent protest or-- if none were happening-- then to add a little spice to the local pillow-fight flash mob.

Thus, for the pragmatic insurgent, if you wanted to meet your 72 virgins in the afterlife fashionably but still required some mobility and functionality, the suicide vests that Salaam D'udsgo Dah'lnarjdad would painstakingly handcraft, simply couldn't be beat.

Crewneck, cropped, tuxedo vests and even puffer vests (for work in the higher altitudes)—all with a soft ballistic lining, of course—were very popular. So much so, Karlattanita's father had subsequently created a brand to reflect their growing popularity.

Each piece of her hazardous handiwork was embossed with their custom label, and All The Rage vests soon became the popular explosive vests in the southwestern provinces.

But, alas, great talent like hers isn't easily ignored, and she-- well into her second year's Spring line (wide pockets en vogue)-- was soon wooed by Madison Avenue with the promise of fame and fortune and a less combustive environment for her and her young daughter.

Little Karla—as she was now known in America—was brought to the States when she was only five, but her father's haunting stories of U.S. imperialism and, worse, the Western world's laziness still were the elements that roiled together like a sooty, black fog, creating horrible nightmares which had kept her company most nights of her life.

But, nowhere has that terror taken a more complete physical form than the store room at the back of her father's anti-American shop. There, that place held the monsters of her darkest dreams.

Years earlier, he'd been re-reading a Donald Trump treatise extolling the virtues of "multi-layered marketing" and "streams of revenue." Flammable flags, it seemed, would not be enough.

"Diversify," the Don had commanded (at a time roughly between his second and third bankruptcies), and her father braved into the effigy business, as well.

Sure, the flags-- of all shapes and sizes-- sold very well but one couldn't count on the constant star that is the anti-West outrage machine.

Witness: the lull in the nineties when there was, regretfully, often far less anger at the U.S. (Thankfully, the rage came back fully when the producers of Baywatch Nights failed to negotiate world-wide syndication rights).

So, since Ahmard the Half-Breed had the only effigy shop in town (and, in truth, it was less like a store and more like a kiosk without the tiny wheels), her father invested in Western-themed cotton-and- papier-mâché depictions of the more deplorable (most popular to be set alight) American figures.

Each had been made carefully by hand (he'd picked up an effigy pattern book off a Farsi-language Amazon knock-off site) and included a money-back guarantee that, when held aloft on its wooden staff (sold separately), the effigy would be fully engulfed in under a minute.

The then-U.S. president initially sold well-- and so did some of the classic presidents (which he'd crafted after sneaking a camera into Florida's "Epcot Center" during a fun-filled weekend one hot July). He'd eventually even branch out into American holidays, representing figures from their Christmas, Thanksgiving, President's Day (see 'classics' note above) and, even, something called "Arbor Day."

How lazy this society that it would celebrate trees?? Her shop-owner father would rage, hands clawing at the sky, then tell her horrific stories of the many, many Western holidays that were steeped in alcohol, dead bird carcasses and capitalism!

Most terrifyingly, he spoke of a man dressed in all red ("Like the Devil himself! A FAT Devil!") who would, perversely, watch over sleeping children, ostensibly to decide if they were or were not to go onto his "killing sheet."

"And, how, how would he choose the children for the slaughter, papa?"

Her father would roll back on his heels, rub his thin beard and say, "Their fate would be sealed if he felt they'd been... naughty!"

She'd gasp.

"You…" her father would often say, recognizing an opportunity (something, as a businessman, he prided himself in) to keep his child in line, "… you haven't been naugh—"

"NO, oh no, father! I am good and of kind heart!"

The following year, when she'd finally come to America with her mother, the celebrated Afghan seamstress, she'd learned the truth about American holidays. Benign, often commercial driven and, sometimes, came with their own seasonal music… but, still, she couldn't shake the nightmares.

As for her mother, Salaam D'udsgo had quickly tired of the cutthroat and volatile nature of the New York fashion scene, eventually settling in rural Wisconsin, making lovely clothing with The Gap for, most notably, a line of knits endorsed by a B-list actress who'd been popular in the eighties (in a fit of irony, one of The Gap's best sellers at the time was a certain forgotten actress' line of sweater-vests).

"I DON'T THINK THAT sounds like a terribly good idea," I said.

We'd, only moments earlier, burst through a door at the bottom of a concrete ramp, hidden at the base of the CDC in Atlanta.

Well, me and Chubbs hadn't actually burst in. We'd been let in by a young woman who said her name was Karla. The two of us had been, in part, chasing Mr. Johnson—the third and oldest Swordsmen. He'd taken the lead on the ramp assault… however, not on purpose.

We'd decided to go all "charge" on the Centers for Disease Control in hopes of finding some left over, non-zombied eggheads working on the cure for the virulent Zombie Bird Flu, which had infected half the country.

However, before then, we'd made a pit stop to the Army surplus store belonging to Charlie the Homophobe (not his Christian name, mind you).

I'd gotten a couple hand grenades and tossed them into my knapsack, but Mr. Johnson had loaded up as if he were going to personally give the Bay of Pigs invasion a solid do-over.

However-- so loaded down with gear-- an hour later, he was running down the ramp, out of control, at full speed and—after Karla thankfully opened the door—he burst inside the complex (instead of the alternative, which was, at the bottom of the ramp, to explode on impact).

Chubbs, my number two man, he was very Zen-spiritual about the whole Saving Mankind Even if it Doesn't Want It thing. He didn't get any weapons from Charles. He'd had his "Octx"-- a pair of crossing-guard stop signs he'd jammed into the flesh of his wrists after losing both of his hands to zombie gullets. His Octx were now where his hands used to be.

And, he was, easily, the best gimp killer of the three of us-- if not on the entire planet.

Now, if you asked him, he'd probably say he was bred that way.

Not purposely trained (or bred) for that particular task, mind you. That hasn't been the plan, per se.

When I'd met Chubbs he was fighting off three very hungry gimps. And given that he'd been bitten and infected like me, he should have changed to be all snarl, "roaahrr", swipe, chomp, chomp... except, yours truly had inadvertently discovered a loophole, which had saved him and me from that particular fate, only the night before.

The previous evening, I'd been bitten by my girlfriend (after she'd become a zombie gimp, but before I'd bashed her zombie brains out with a small, tin frog band decoration), and then stumbled over to a nearby pharmacy intent on overdosing on pain medicine.

Like anyone half-paying attention, I'd seen what becoming a zombie meant. I didn't like it nor its unparalleled affinity for 24-7 interstate commuting.

Seeking the deathly effects of a fist-full of pain meds, I'd instead inadvertently grabbed handfuls of medicine designed to treat erectile dysfunction—and, it turns out, with that wee bit of blood redirected away from the brain, that keeps the Full Zombie effects at bay.

We are instead, as I call it, Near Zombie (NZ), imbued with some of the nicer gimp qualities (heightened senses, stronger... uh... strength) while foregoing the social faux pas of god-I'm-famished-how-about-that-human-leg-you-are-standing-on.

And, of course, being ED medicine, we three are also, well, permanently erect.

Yes, we are the ones you've heard of.

We are the turgid.

We are The Swordsmen.

ONCE WE'D FINALLY RUN at a respectable clip seeking out Mr. Johnson (who'd appeared to have taken a turn down a hallway we hadn't), Karla had us at a full sprint again, heading deeper into the complex.

"My girls are up, just north-east of here about a hundred fifty yards," she told us, panting. "They got pinned down. Me and three others got out and we were trying to circle back around. The other two," she said, closed her eyes for a moment, "They got nabbed. I tried…"

"Uh," I said, "Yes, very distressing to hear. But our man-- the old guy-- which way do you think he went?"

She wiped her mouth, her breath turning hoarse, and said, "He'll be fine over here, on this side. They've abandoned this area-- we took it from them. We'll circle back, I swear it."

Chubbs stared at her, eyes a little distant, just nodding.

Still, the thought of leaving a man behind even for just a moment…

Karla must have sensed my hesitation. She slowed, then stopped. Turning to me, eyes a little wild, she said: "I promise no harm will come to him. Please, help me!"

Tears began to bubble up on her lower lids and I offered, "Okay, I'm going to trust you. But keep in mind-- the last woman to violate my trust got a tin frog band slammed into her Premotor Cortex."

Her eyes turned to slits and she said, "Premot…? Ah, ha! I saw you looking that up on your phone a minute ago."

"What? No."

"Yes, you did," she said pointing to my pocket. "I looked over and you had a color-coded brain diagram on the little screen. Do you mean to tell me you were planning that little speech--"

"Listen, listen! Do you want to argue or save your girls, now??" I said, getting to more important matters. "We're willing to help, and you can't do it alone. I mean, not much you can do sometimes all 'Party of One, thank you very much.' Frankly, I'm surprised you haven't been infected already."

We took a hard turn, kept running.

In the distance, we could hear machine gun fire. And, I swear, on occasion, what sounded like mortar rounds.

"Oh, I'm infected. All the ladies are."

Chubbs chimed in, "But then how—"

She grinned and tugged at her shirt. That face I'd seen when first coming into the complex, now, was once again staring back at me.

"I… I was going to ask about that."

IT TURNS OUT, RATHER obviously, that ED meds, they're not going to work on the ladies. And if it did happen to work on a certain lady or two, well, you may need to broaden your definition of the word "lady."

But, in principle, the "process" still worked.

Bluntly, getting one's pink parts flushed with blood— more specifically, getting that bit of blood away from the brain—that seemed to be a key to hang in the Near Zombie (NZ) area rather than Full Zombie (FZ).

And, if there isn't an ED medicine for women (no gents there ain't no Spanish Fly. Really. Despite what you may read on the Internet)—they have to become aroused, permanently as possible, in other ways.

"So, all of you—"

"Yes," she said.

"All your girls, you guys have t-shirts with, uh..."

"Russell Brand on them, yes."

I started to talk again but she turned to me and gave me a finger to the lips, pushing down with her other hand.

This, obviously, was her "shush and stop running" look. She must've been working on that one. Because I knew right away it was a "shush and stop running." Raw talent this one. She would interest me, so.

Chubbs had not been privy to the "shush and stop running" finger/Madonna-vogue thing she'd done and nearly banged into me from behind.

The hallway we'd turned down was tinier than the previous, I realized, as the deeper we got inside the CDC complex we began to leave arteries, moving then onto veins and eventually capillaries.

Instantly, I regretted that analogy, now stuck in my head.

But before I could properly shoo it away-- or at least give my head a good couple shakes to see if I could clear it via the tried and true Etch-a-Sketch method-- an incredible sccccrreeeeetttccchhhh!! burst all around me.

"Sorry," Chubbs said, apologizing because he'd had to use his Octx, his stop sign hands, along the walls to slow down.

At least I think that's what he'd apologized for.

He'd come up real close behind me and given his "compass forever points north" like mine, I wondered if I'd missed some brief, panicked, errant personal violation (or if I were just blocking it).

I don't have any problem with guys that do that sort of thing, but I don't want to be one of them. And the hetro-code pretty much would have meant, me and Chubbs would have to shake hands, go our separate ways, and never speak about it again to anyone but a certified mental health professional.

"Seriously?" Karla growled at Chubbs and he looked down. Don't know why he did and don't want to know. Moving on.

She then held both her hands up and blinked really slow: Don't move, be quiet, I'm listening.

God, she was good.

Sure enough, she was NZ like me and Chubbs were-- and with it, she had a very keen sense of hearing. Better than even mine, it seemed.

Because, moments later, I finally heard it.

Huf huf huf huf huf-- "Titties!"-- jingle, jingle, clap.

Behind me, I hear Chubbs get into his fighting stance-- his Octx slicing through the air as if he were sharpening them against the dark air.

"What the hell--"

Before she can finish her thought, a low, concussive thunder rolls through the complex. As the momentary shaking fades, dirt, grit and moth snot falls from the cracks in the ceiling above (yes, I can smell that stuff! Very blechy!)

"-- was that?"

"Which one?"

"I think," Chubbs offered. "The jingly banging sound that said 'titties,' that was Mr. Johnson. He's on our side but he's a nasty old dude."

Oh damn.

"What's wrong?"

I blinked at Karla. "What do you mean 'what's wrong?'"

"Dunno," she said and motioned us to start moving down the hall again, slower now. "You had an 'oh damn' face a second ago. So I asked what was wrong..."

Whoa. This girl was good.

And she was right. I was worried.

"I've got some grenades in this pack strapped to me," I said as we started trotting. Another low boom but we kept going-- heading toward it.

Which as loud noises go, in human evolution theory, you're supposed to go in the opposite direction.

(There are two notable exceptions when one is to turn away from something loud, in my book-- 1: On the rare chance a stranger may yell, "Goodness! They've just pulled actress Jennifer Connelly from the pool! Has anyone seen CPR performed on television so many times that they believe they may have actually acquired that particular skill?!?"... and 2: If someone has just called out "Marco").

Behind me Chubbs was trotting and humming but, thankfully, he was keeping it low (for now).

"Good, we'll need 'em," Karla said and took another corner. She slowed-- the light in this hallway had been

smashed. There was a splash of fluorescent at the far end--
another hallway-- but we'd be in the dark until then.

"Well, no. I mean, yes," I said. "Grenades will likely
become very handy in the next, oh, minute and a half... but
what's next to the grenades."

Chubbs sucked in a breath.

"Oh fuuuck. He needs a re-dose?"

She looked over her shoulder, popped her eyebrows.

I said, "Next to the handful of grenades in my knapsack
is our entire stash of ED medicine. It's all that will keep the
three of us Swordsmen from crossing over to Full Zombie."

As we approached the dim, flickering light, we began to
hear voices. Even though they were distant, their tone could
not be mistaken: panicked, hurried, desperate.

Karla stopped, put her hand against the wall to catch
her breath.

Chubbs, for as heavy as he was, looked like he could
run another hundred miles. He went up ahead ten feet,
looked down the hall.

"Your man is out of meds, right?"

I nodded.

"But, hold up," Chubbs said, walking back to us-- one
eye still on the corner. "He's got his own meds with that
patch thingy, right?"

Karla scrunched up her face, "Ick, he's on an ED
patch??"

Chubbs agreed, grinning a little strangely at her: "Tell
me about it."

"Was," I said. "He was getting dosed through a patch. But it's a week supply and today is day seven."

"Damn."

"Yeah, I dropped a handful of Blues into his shirt pocket but with all the guns and stuff he's strapped on, I don't know if he can get to it."

Karla took a couple steps forward toward the corner and said, "Oh, right."

Chubbs had missed it.

"So, he doesn't know it but I think he may be taking a page out of your book. You with your horrible t-shirt."

"It's not horrible!" she said. "This man is a gorgeous, golden god to many ladies. He's smart, he's tender, he a wounded soul. And Russell's got the funny-sexy thing--"

"ALL right already," I said. "Enough. I got it."

Karla added, "He's the sexiest man alive."

"Whoa, whoa, hold on now," I warned her. "I believe we need to leave that up to People magazine's annual declarative issue. Time-honored. Certified. So, no jumping the gun. There is a process in place, let it happen on its own."

Chubbs got it now (despite the odd banter between me and Karla).

"Oh, he was saying and thinking about 'titties' to keep himself from turning FZ."

I shrugged. "Gotta hand it to him. Whatever works."

Turning back to Karla, I noticed-- keenly-- that she'd gone. I looked at Chubbs and, strangely, he looked back the way we'd come. Then she called out, just ahead around the corner--

"Come on, we're nearly there."

"THERE," IT TURNS OUT, was something just this side of the Battle of fucking Waterloo.

The use of that particular harmless word-- "there"-- should be reserved for simple, demonstrative speech. As in:

"Where are the muffins the Anderson's brought to this nice backyard picnic?"

 "Oh, their muffins? They're over there."

See? Simple, easy, safe word.

But as we rounded the last corner-- this, at the end of a long, long hall that dropped with a grade usually reserved for either slowing runaway semis or handicap entrances-- it was like we'd crossed over the top of a professional football stadium, now getting our first look inside.

"Oh my… just…"

"Yeah," I said to Chubbs. "We are definitely going to die."

TO BE HONEST, I felt we'd been pretty malleable since the moment Karla had swung the CDC's ramp door open for us. Yes, sure, The Swordsmen would have been steak tar-tar for the zombie masses had she not been there but a guy's gotta have his limits.

And, don't forget-- we had a plan heading into the CDC, right?

Then this pretty girl comes along and poof! it all goes up in smoke? Our master plan is put on the backburner while we are led around by the nose by some, what?, twenty-something girl in tight leather, packing twin modified AK-47s?

And who do you know that's got shiny leather? All slick and curvy. Hell, I bet she oiled it up! This while her embattled "Ladies" face near certain death!

Deep breath.

It was just the dose talking.

I'd been on a 24-hour regimen of boner medicine-- that's why I'd been so easily swayed by a sexy girl with olive skin, eyes like the Dead Sea, wrapped in tanned leather and strapped with assault rifles!

Then, I realized-- no, that hadn't been the ED meds talking.

A man's plans upended, changed beyond recognition, and he simply, willingly awaits the next whim of a pretty girl?

Nah, that wasn't the meds.

That was 250,000 years of evolution talking.

Still, I wanted some answers (and, hell, if she'd give me those answers in a low, husky voice-- every other sentence addressing me as "big daddy"-- who was I to complain. She didn't, mind you. And I didn't ask (see above: re, twin AK47s).

"Come on," Karla said, her stark green eyes flashing in the half-light. She took a couple steps forward, then turned back. "What the hell are you doing?"

Chubbs, my wingman, leaned up against the concrete wall, arms crossed, Octx tap-tap-a-tapping. He gave me a nod that said You the man (as I've said, I'm terrible at interpreting non-vocal signals-- and even worse at expressing them-- so I have no idea what he was really saying. But, I'm going with You the man because that's what I needed to hear at the moment, frankly).

Below us was a firefight.

A battle.

And totally surreal.

I learned later that day this entire area had been part of a mine, back in the late eighteenth, early nineteenth century. And, carved so deep into the rock and hard Georgia clay, it remained this deep, empty chasm.

So much so that the Underground Railroad had even run through here at one point.

At least that's what the sun-bleached brochure for the "Walking Tour of the Underground Railroad" had claimed.

Like I said, below us was like looking down on a football stadium... but a Roman coliseum would have been more correct.

Dirt and rock floor, uneven.

Walls that had been blasted out by TNT a hundred years earlier, uneven, rock scooped away like cavities in the mouth of some child giant with an affinity for Skittles.

And, a little incongruously, hundreds of broken and busted up pieces of office furniture: ergonomic chairs, conference room tables, filing cabinets...

On our left, below, was inexplicably the armed wing of the WWF. Yeah, the panda people.

Remember when the other WWF went head to head with them?

As in the World Wrestling Federation. A hundred muscle-ripped dudes hopped up on overinflated ego, anabolic steroids and human growth hormone?

Yeah.

THEY backed down from these guys. Changed their name to the, blah, the WWE? WWE? Sounds like some Robert Bly nature outing for those with speech impediments.

So should we have been worried? I mean human muscle mutants were afraid of the WWF!

So... yes.

My jaw clenched, I asked her: "What the hell have you gotten us into?"

Karla looked panicked. She was ready to breach the lines of the armed WWF agents attacking her people but needed our help.

And I felt for her, really did. But I needed to know, at that moment, anything what-so-ever about what the flying fuck was going on around me!!!

She blinked slowly.

"Okay, okay," she said and raised her hands, cast from fingertip to elbow with leather (oiled???) gloves. "Can we at least start moving toward my dying friends?"

Chubbs gave me the nod and we headed downward.

It was a descent of fits and starts. There may have been a path at some point but this was an area, it seemed, over the years that had been rife with conflict-- the battle below was not the first to take place in this giant cavern.

Thankfully, there were thick ropes threaded through stanchions that had been hammered securely into the rock beneath us. We went hand over hand much of the way, slowly making our way lower and lower toward the battle.

The smell of cordite, the concussive waves hitting my chest deeper and deeper the lower we climbed, something in me didn't care about why we were there anymore.

I was ready for the fight.

(That, I think, was about the ED medicine. Cause I would have lay into a rotting pumpkin at that point-- at least shooting at panda people might take the edge off).

Karla pointed off to her right-- the WWF agents were taking ground toward the shipping dock. At the back of the advancing force, a woman in a golf cart. Sitting next to her, the driver was a small man with circular spectacles and a clipboard.

Yeah... I know evil when I see it.

"You're not talking," I reminded her between deep breaths.

"This is a hard climb down, Hal!"

"That's 'General,' Karla," Chubbs said (and thankfully didn't explain my namesake). "A little respect, huh?"

She spun back and gave him a look but it quickly melted into a small smile and, I swear, she blushed a little.

"Sorry, Chubby-man."

I'd gone slow for my Number Two because ol' boy didn't have any hands to speak of. His stoppy-sign Octx were perfect for gimp killing... but real crap much of anything else.

Part of him, I could tell, was trying to shirk off my help-- he was trying to manage on his own. But we were a team-- had each other's backs (or hands) when needed.

I held onto the grimy ropes, hand over hand, taking steps quickly but not too quickly, and Chubbs finally just put his Octx on each of my shoulder blades and held as tight as he could until the terrain flattened out.

"At the start-- and I don't know when that was-- they were pissed," Karla said, huffing as she maneuvered over a jagged, rocky patch. Her voice oscillated between a hoarse whisper and full-throated yelling-- depending upon the volume of blasts below us.

"Who is they?" Chubbs asked.

"The WWF people," she said motioning to the agents in the black jumpers below us who were firing assault rifles at her friends. "Humans had been experimenting on animals for years, of course. Animal testing for drugs, products, shampoos, whatever."

"I never thought them to be very concerned about that," I said and a blast below us shook the ground.

Two of her Ladies fell. She looked away.

"We're close," I offered. "In about a minute, we can split off and take them from behind."

Karla's demeanor spun on a dime; her eyes widened and a sexy little grin pulled the corners of her mouth upward.

"My, my, General but you do say the naughtiest things."

"Wha...? No, no... I mean-- there, if we-- what?"

She laughed-- actually laughed (and in this hell, you had to admire her for it)-- then waved me off.

A moment later BOOM! and we all dropped to the ground. Bits of rock and dirt rained down upon us.

That hadn't been stray fire: someone had taken a pot-shot at us.

We'd been spotted.

She continued, "The trucks there and the WWF force trying to get to them? You're looking at what they call Project Darwin."

Chubbs shook his head, "Man, I don't like the sound of that. My family is very Catholic."

Karla stopped her decent and pulled at a couple of straps-- both of her modified assault weapons dangled freely. She checked her mags as she spoke.

"A couple years ago, there'd been this sort of three-card-monty shuffling of money."

Finally, I asked, "How do you know this?"

She smiled weakly, nodded her head down to her Ladies.

"We used to work for the CDC. Got privy to some files about what was really going on but, maybe, too late."

"You worked--? Are you scientists?"

Karla shook her head, eyes cast down. "Nope. They-- nice folks, too, all of them-- they're all gone, as far as I can tell. We were part of their production house. We made commercials, industrial films."

Chubbs stiffened, "The propaganda wing!"

"Yes, comrade Chubbs," she said and smiled at him. He melted and that was the end of any challenge to her from Swordsmen Number Two for the rest of the day.

Another close explosion.

"We gotta split up," Karla said. "I'll go around the side and try and see if I can reach my friends. You bugger these assholes from behind, as you so delightfully put it," she yelled over the blasts below us. Her face went mock-serious and she added, "I mean, if that's all right with you, General."

I nodded, but if me and Chubbs were about to die I felt we had to know why.

"What is Project Darwin?"

She thought for a moment, then chuckled.

"Gotta hand it to them. They really do believe in their work, you know. Protecting wildlife and all that," she said and pulled back the stocks on both weapons, balanced under her arms. "The collective wisdom they acted upon-- the driving goal behind Project Darwin-- is based on the insight... or lunacy... that the only way humans are going to live harmonious with animals is if we... well, dialed it back a couple hundred millennia."

Hell no.

"What?"

"Yeah, Project Darwin is what you see down there in those trucks. Loaded up with meds-- disguised as male impotence medicine and breast enhancement tablets."

Maybe I'd been off about my theory, why the meds had prevented me from becoming one of the undead. That would have to wait.

"Why those pills?"

She shrugged and said, "Because they're the real top sellers around the world. And doctors don't blink twice when shelling them out." She edged away from us slowly, toward her team. "And the guys in black down there-- they believe that for humans to truly live in balance with nature and the animals around them-- well, that means taking humans back to, oh, the human erectus era." She laughed as she turned, and called over her shoulder.

And the next part, I'm not entirely clear on, since she was moving away and it was so very, very, very loud. Much booming and banging going on around us (And, as a side note, her butt was framed so lovely in her oily leather pants. I missed most of what she'd said... but it was something like--)

"Ha, not the erectus you Swordsmen have brought upon yourself. But rather de-evolving mankind. Back to the caves and like that."

Chubbs tapped me on the shoulder-- we were a little exposed, and it was time to make our way down.

"What do you mean back to the caves, Karla?" Chubbs yelled over the assault-- not only about a hundred yards from where we stood. "You seriously mean they think the only way we'll be all 'harmonious' with nature is making us-- what?-- friggin' cavemen again?"

She shrugged, and her hair flipped just so as she did, then said, "Of course, now, the ZBF? Zombie Bird Flu? That was just Beta testing gone wrong. The gimps, man... they'll die out," she said and pointed to the docks. "And if that shipment gets onto the streets, and subsequent ones like it, and into the hands of everyday people-- all CDC and FDA certified-- it'll be only a matter of months before that happens.."

"That can't be true," I said, barely above a whisper.

"The human race will be like one big, extras pool for a remake of Quest for Fire, man. It'll be a quarter million years before we ever see an episode of American Idol again."

Looking down at the explosions, the bodies piling up below us-- but thinking about what she'd just said, I replied:

"I don't think you're making a terribly good argument against Project Darwin, Karla. You know... just fyi."

NOW, DESPITE BEING HUNG with the moniker "General," it should come as no surprise to you that I don't know a damn thing about battlefield tactics.

However, I did once, years ago, read Art of War.

And, full admission, I didn't actually read Art of War, but instead listened to the book on tape. Adding to the degrees of separation, a friend of mine had given me the CD after she'd downloaded it from a torrent pirating website in the UK.

I only found out, years later, after the owner of the website had been arrested in an FBI/MI5/KGB/ASPCA sting operation that the audio books on the website were not, in fact, pirated at all.

The webmaster had been some Belfast kid in his mid-twenties that wanted to be a radio DJ but had trouble passing the drug screen (note: we don't have that here in the U.S. If we did, you'd only hear white noise... on every channel... in every city... around the country).

So, instead, he'd simply bought a cheap mike and recorded himself reading the book on tape and passed it off as an audio book.

In fact, it had been that little hitch, that technicality, which had saved him from being prosecuted.

He walked away from the trial a free man. However, and incredibly, he was found in Madrid three months later, gored to death during Spain's annual Running. This tragedy had come as a complete surprise to everyone, especially given that the festival actually takes place in Pamplona, 250 miles away.

That aside, my education from The Art of War-- written by a dead Chinese general and read to me by a dead, stoned Irishman-- had been used mainly, I am somewhat ashamed to admit, rather "off label."

I'd taken the rules of defeating a wartime opponent, cherished for thousands of years, and used them to get girls.

For example:

Appear weak when you are strong, and strong when you are weak.
        --Sun Tzu, The Art of War
Became...

Agree with everything she says, and she may eventually sleep with you.
        --Sun Hal, The Art of Her

Another example:

The supreme art of war is to subdue the enemy without fighting.

--Sun Tzu, The Art of War

Which I'd retooled as...

Cry sometimes You could get pity sex out of it.
        --Sun Hal, The Art of Her

Listen, I'm not proud of what I'd done, all those years ago, because (in part) I'd not done anything.

While ol' Gordon Gecko had championed these rules of war as a business guide back in the eighties (leading wall-plasterings of his words hung up in alpha-male, asshole college dorms around the country) the book actually did very little for me when put to my practical use.

Except, as an aside, the amateur hour audio version did help me learn to fake an Irish accent a little.

And that little nugget (a story for another time) worked out just dandy a couple wonderful, dizzying times, lassie.

OH, before I move on, here's one last one:

Even the finest sword plunged into salt water will eventually rust."
        --Sun Tzu, The Art of War

Then, becomes...

Wrap it before you tap it.
        --Sun Hal, The Art of Her

Not really a relevant get-some tip but just good advice. That's one for the kids.

Okay, moving on.

IT IS SAID FRANCIS Scott Key wrote the cherished American anthem, The Star-Spangled Banner, while "bombs bursting in air" all around him.

But, as Chubbs and I got to level ground faced with countless black-clad and heavily armed WWF agents, a rocket-propelled-grenade blasted a small file cabinet into dust, so I was fighting simply not to soil the only pair of pants I had left in the world.

"Jeez, man," Chubbs said as he struggled to get back up off the ground, jamming his Octx into the rock and dirt as he did. "Now I wish I would have loaded up with a boomstick or something."

Between the two of us, it appeared they'd worked out which one was the greater threat and had aimed at my friend.

A second WWF agent was lifting an RPG launcher to his shoulder and I didn't need to trace his eyes to see where shot two was going to go. Chubbs hadn't completely gotten back up, a little shell-shocked and was a sitting duck.

"Chubbs, you're out in the open a bit. Move it, man!"

He wobbled again and was up on his toes, but the agent was ready to deliver.

That, I wasn't going to let that happen.

There were grenades in my bag, but no time to pull them out, yank the pin and toss at a target.

"General, I'm… gimme a sec."

Chubbs' calf was bloodied but it wasn't bad. He started hobbling toward a small pile of mangled executive desks. No way he'd get there in time and even if he did, the splinters from the desks would likely slice through every inch of his body.

Turning toward the cluster of agents, only about fifty feet away from us, I swung around the firing catch that led to a small pack strapped to my thigh.

Clutching the trigger, I heard the nitrogen gas punch the liquid in the adjacent chamber, sending it twisting and churning up its hose. As the fuel passed the catch and up to the igniter, I'd already squeezed out a nice spark for it.

"Gentlemen," I yelled, aiming my nozzle at the wide-eyed agents. "Say hello to my little flame!"

The dim, steely light around us was suddenly burning white-hot by the sun flare that burst from the flamethrower I'd gotten from Charlie the Homophobe hours earlier.

Standing in a fighting stance, legs apart, and protecting my friend by washing our enemy down with a river of flame, my only thought was Holy shit, my eyebrows are on fire!

"All right, General!" Chubbs called out triumphantly.

At least nine uniformed fighters of the small regiment nearest to us were now lit up and burning, running, hitting each other and generally out of commission.

The one that had been ready to fire his RPG at Chubbs, that guy exploded, blasting four others-- including the two not on fire-- into gooey bits of people stuff which sizzled and snapped as it landed on the flaming WWF foot soldiers running around them in circles.

"Hal, here," Chubbs found a solid space behind an outcropping of rock. "Back here!"

Taking a few steps back, I scanned the smoke and fire to see if one was readying itself for a little payback. What I did see, instead, was a woman standing in a battle-ready golf cart, binoculars lifted toward me.

My NZ senses sharpened, I probably could see her as well as she could see me.

I couldn't see a face but knew that was their commander.

It had been her job to get those trucks out and on the road, but had to cut down Karla's Ladies if she were to do it.

And now she had to fight two fronts-- she hadn't expected that and seemed totally unprepared.

All these years later-- at least a small, small victory at that point-- I had to hand it to Sun Tzu after. For it was he who said:

If the hot girl at the bar is outta your league, don't bother. If not, remember: chicks dig jerks. And, most importantly, get her away from her homely, c-blocking friend.

Ah, nope, hold on. That's actually my retooled version. Here's the original:

If your enemy is superior, evade. If angry, irritate. If not equally matched, split your enemy and revaluate.
    --Sun Tzu, The Art of War

Actually, as I read that back, it seems I got it entirely wrong.

Hmm.

Instead of splitting the enemy, we'd split ourselves.

And, if my man Sunny knew what he was talking about... that misstep would turn out to be a very bad idea.

The group near us out of the picture (but impressively still screaming and burning a little), two regiments of about a half dozen WWF agents a piece were heading toward us.

Now, the very good part was they were also heading away from Karla's Ladies. And as I looked over, she seemed to be edging her away toward being able to flank a couple agents who were lobbing smoke grenades into the truck docks.

But, to be clear, the very bad part was that-- as I mentioned-- they were heading toward us.

So... Good: not killing Karla et al.

Bad: they were coming to kill us.

In the end, a wash, I suppose.

Unless, of course, we could stop them from killing us. And Chubbs and me were all for that.

"Get back here, General!" he yelled as a small, fist sized object arched over where he was holed up, but then got caught up on a rock lip. He was right-- that was a good position. Not only fortified on the side and front, but up top.

Looking across the cavern, past the smoke, I could see Karla take a shot at two black-clad WWF'ers and put them down. But a couple others were coming up behind her.

She hadn't seen them.

"Karl--!"

.......?

.... wha?... did?...

At this distance, there isn't any chance she can hear me. What is that ringing, now?

It, hmm, hmm, still can't seem to...

And, now, all doesn't feel right with the world. Someone, they threw something at me.

Yep.

Yes. That's it.

Hit me with something.

Oh, now I see it! Someone threw a friggin' leg at me? Who throws full limbs at their opponents?

My eyes are all sparkly, why can't I see straight?

Wait a minute now-- the first time I saw Chubbs, hey, you know, he'd thrown a leg at me!

That means... I'd been attacked with a decapitated leg twice in one day???

Whoops, I'm falling.

slowly

slowly

Slowly to the soft, pillow-y rocks below.

Then, I can see a little better and, hey, notice the guy who'd thrown his leg at me had the exact same pair of high-top Converse tennis shoes I do!

Oh, oh... mhmmm. Wars are bad. Here is an "enemy" of mine, enemy mine, but if we both like the chucks, why can't we be fri--

"Hal!"

Totally like in the U.S. Civil War, brother against-- ow, that hurt mah shoulder-- against brother. War, what is it good for?

Not a lot.

Nope.

"Hal!"

Chubbs is suddenly over me, which is weird, because that says to me that he can fly!

And, whoa, I'm just finding out now? Some fr--

"Come on, General," he says to me, all swirly like. "I can't pull you unless you grab on!"

OH, he can use his stoppy hands to fly? Cool. I got get me a pair of--

BLAM!

"Wow," I said and my mind was suddenly back in my head again.

"Let's go, let's go!" Chubbs said, his eyes darting from me, then back toward the horizon, then back to me.

"You hit me with your Octx, didn't you?"

Breathing heavy, he tried to get me moving, saying: "Grab a hold and I'll pull ya, Hal. We got about twenty-five feet, we can make it."

Whoa, I was so tired-- and everything felt like waking up from a dream. As if my mind had drifted away and now slowly drizzled back through a hole at the top of my head like it'd been pulverized into some sort of brain batter.

Blechy.

Chubbs was great, pulling me along as I held tight to his Octx. My eyes were beginning to uncross a little-- a good thing-- but as they did I saw a line of black uniforms, all emblazoned with that hateful little panda symbol.

The WWF agents were closing in fast.

And with Chubbs pulling me, how the hell could he fight a half dozen of these guys at the same time?

Surprised that being dragged across the rocks and dirt didn't really hurt, or feel like anything at all, I looked up at his face and saw he was panicked. Protecting me, he was risking his life.

Again.

Then I remembered!

"Grenades!"

Digging into my knapsack that was hanging askew, off of my right elbow now, I reached in and pulled one out... one good throw and--

"Damn," I said. "I only got the pin. Well, that's not going to hurt anybody."

Chubbs stopped pulling and his head snapped back.

He said: "What'd you just say?"

Preliminary Incident Report #101712sm

Date: October 17th
Supervisor Requesting Audit: F.M. Janice Kutler
Account of: D. Stinnett, Servicemember 2ndary
Div. (unverified)

   This report is to detail the event that led
to [**REDACTED**] in the clearest detail I can
recall.

   Before [**REDACTED**] but after [**REDACTED**], my
regiment had been commanded to advance up the
south-southwest wall of the conflict toward the
two men who'd [**REDACTED**] only moments earlier.
   Note: that particular incident left a sort
of sickly barbeque smell wafting through the air.
Human barbeque.
   Which, of course, despite the unpleasant
nature of that observation, fully explains why I
was doubled over and spilling the contents of my
stomach between a couple office chairs and a
piling of rocks when the others advanced past me.
   Had I known [**REDACTED**], but I don't expect
something like that to make it into the final
report so won't bother detailing further.
   The disputed event occurred, it's important
to point out, just seconds before I was knocked
unconscious.
   This is to only serve as a warning that the
very few memories I have of that moment are as if
made of paraffin wax…   What is clear is that
the rest of my team was moving forward, weapons
ready, and I'd done my best to catch up after the
wave of nausea had passed.
   I'd heard one of them shout something.
   Not in anger, but, and I can only guess,
he'd sounded resigned, if I were to hazard a
guess.

Then, I looked toward him. And then looked up just above us.

And that's when, as I've explained numerous times, the kid's knapsack flew toward the rest of my battalion and, in a moment of brilliant light and sound, it exploded, killing every one of my team and knocking me unconscious.

I would hope the WWF Executive Council will ultimately see my compliance, and innocence, in this matter.

SSD Stinnett

Addendum (Oct. 18th): I don't expect this matters, but I had promised to detail everything I could remember. And, despite how odd it seems, I'd gone in and out of consciousness, so I expect this was some sort of hallucination-- but as they slipped away, it seemed… well, it seemed as though one of the men was carrying his own leg.

AS I'VE SAID, SO much can be expressed (and far more quickly, and completely, than using words) in just a gesture or facial expression.

After I'd said, "I only got the pin. Well, that's not going to hurt anybody" Chubbs dropped a look on me that said either, Did you hear?? Free buffet at Golden Corral! or You've got a live grenade in your knapsack!

So, with all the strength I'd had left, I'd thrown the knapsack as far as possible.

This incidentally, and even karmically maybe, turned out to be in the direction of the half dozen attackers advancing toward us at that moment.

In a blast that rings my ears a little even to this day, it flattened this group, even the one in the back, who appeared to be covered in vomit.

Chubbs had pulled us back to his hole-in-the-rock, and I knew that we had another group coming in at us from the other flank but, man, just couldn't seem to get my footing.

"Because you're missing a leg, Hal."

"That would explain it," I said. Looking down, sure enough, I had half a pair of pants. "The blast that knocked me down, then, huh?"

Chubbs gave me a weak smile, shook his head.

"Nah, actually, you bad-ass, you were upright through the blast," he said. Then cast a look around the corner. "But the explosion sent this keyboard shelf slicing through the air."

I nodded. Yep.

"And slicing through my Levis."

The echoes of assault rifles, pistols and grenades' snap-boom sounded like war's symphony around us. Chubbs seemed more worried about me than the approaching WWF agents, who had to be just seconds away from overrunning our position.

Sure, I'd seen enough bad TV medical dramas to know that my body was numb with shock. But, I never thought it'd be so... chill.

Which, as an evolutionary survival component, it seems we got the design a bit cross-wired.

Because, when we're hit with something so overpowering it puts us into a mental and physical shock, how much better would it be if we went all David-Banner-oh-no-you-di'int on whatever danger present, right?

But instead of going all Hulk, I felt more, Hey, you guys wanna get some chips, and we'll dim the lights, lounge around in beanbags and watch all the Lord of the Rings movies back to back? How about, huh?

Maybe it was just me.

Maybe I wasn't the warrior for Saving All Mankind Even the Australians.

Chubbs, however, this guy, he was a Zen master, fighting, rodeo clown.

Good dude.

"What?" he said.

"Nothing," I yelled back, over the blasts. He'd taken position just inside our rock aperture, casting glances over his shoulder at me. Slowly, I felt myself coming from out of the fog. "How's Karla?"

Chubbs ducked and something ricocheted passed him, rock dust spit from the back wall.

"They're holding, I think," he said. "But there's only three trucks left."

Using my elbows, I sat up.

"Great! They took out the other two?"

My friend shook his head. "They're out on the road. Gone, man."

"Shit. We gotta help her stop the other three."

Another huge blast rained pebbles down on both of us.

"Hal, we're gonna try," Chubbs said. "But at this point, I'm just focused on all of us getting out of here intact." He said then flickered his eyes back to where my left leg had been. "Well, at least, you know, mostly intact."

I wasn't sitting out the fight just because my leg was gone. For one, being Near Zombie, it didn't really hurt much.

Two, I sorta wanted some payback for it.

By the time Chubbs looked back to me again, I was holding the wall, hopping along. He smiled, nodded slowly.

"Let's do this rodeo-clown," I said.

He laughed.

"General, you don't have much fuel left in the flamer and all your grenades are out there, blown up."

They blew up-- he didn't say, but we both thought it-- with the ED meds that kept us both from crossing over into undead territory.

We'd dosed before heading into the CDC but how long would that last?

I gave my chest a one-two punch and said, "I still got me spikes. You got your Octx."

"That's right," Chubbs nodded, then his eyes flared. "Damn right!"

"Come on, man," I said and grabbed his shoulder this time. "Let's give these guys a seriously deadly freak show!"

"Murderous, General!"

Be both leapt out, Chubbs in his fighting stance, red-bladed hands at the ready and me with flame thrower cocked, another hand on the spike sticking out of my left pec.

"Wow," my Number Two said as he took in the sight in front of us.

"Hey, where'd they get all the extra guys from?"

Chubbs and I stood there ready to do battle with the six WWF agents who were now about thirty feet away.

And just behind them, another three regiments of six to eight a piece and along the other wall another dozen.

Each had an assault rifle and flack gear. Each regiment had at least one agent carrying a rocket-propelled grenade launcher.

We had two bloodied stop signs, two rusted railroad spikes, about twenty seconds of flame and--

Huf huf huf!

--not much else.

But, despite each of us...

huf huf huf!

being down a limb or more...

jingle, jingle, clap, clap!

We were going to give him whatever hell we had.

Fwwwwwwt-- BOOM!

The Earth shook as if god had sneezed, and we braced for impact but instead, to our right, the middle of the WWF regiment on the far wall turned to ash and entrails.

Our surprise was reflected back on the face of the closest WWF agent to us.

"Wait, if that's not them," I said. "Hey, maybe Karla--"

Another teeth numbing blast and the front half of that regiment was obliterated, gone. The remaining three were now in full retreat.

"Hell ya!" Chubbs yelled and smiled. He snapped his head in the opposite direction, and pointed upward like Casey-At-The-Bat. "General!"

Up about fifty feet, from the opening where we'd come in, that had been the source of the attack.

Smoke twisted with dust, and in the dark, too hard to see but then I heard a voice yell and split the air:

"Angela Lansbury's puss-say!"

A moment later, a line of smoke leapt from the clouded opening like a lizards tongue down to the three agents left and when it got there, the small missile destroyed what had remained of the regiment.

"Yes!" Chubbs yelled. "Mr. Johnson, you creepy, nasty old son-of-bitch! Love that guy!"

Johnson put a fist in the air-- not all the way up-- he was still pretty weighted down. "Motorrr-boating Elizabeth Taylor!"

I shrugged and said to my friend. "Whatever works, man."

The agents to our left saw an opportunity and quickened their advance-- they were nearly on us now.

Chubbs looked down at them, back up to Mr. Johnson who fifty-feet up and a hundred-fifty yards away.

The eldest of our Swordsman was pacing side to side, craning his neck.

"Why... why won't he blast 'em?"

"He can't," I said. Shaking my head. "From there, he'd just as likely hit us. We're directly in the line of sight."

Chubbs' elation turned back to anger and, he couldn't hide it, a little fear.

"What... what do we do?"

The agents inched forward, over the uneven rock, dirt and furniture terrain.

"General, what do we do?"

My mind went back to Sun Tzu, but then I remembered his words of wisdom had never once worked for me. Sure, they hadn't been what the guy intended, so I had to cut him some slack.

But, if those who know me know anything-- I've always got one really stupid idea left in me.

"Get my leg!"

"What?" Chubbs yelled back and I nodded quickly. Then, all-in because he had to be, he ran down the drag marks in the dirt toward my limb lying in the dirt.

An RPG flew past his head, narrowly missing, and exploded on the far wall. Another shower of tiny rock.

Seconds later, he handed it back but by this time, I'd hopped my way about fifteen feet away from the opening of the hiding place.

"Hey, get--"

"Nah, let's give this a shot," I said, then called out as loud as I could to Mr. Johnson. "Here!"

He looked down, and I could see him squinting.

"HERE!" I yelled, then yelled again. "At me!"

The first agent breached our area, a flat shelf in the rock about as large as a backyard pool.

Chubbs got to him before he could train the rifle on either of us.

Slice, dice, head went-a-rollin'.

And as it did, Chubbs took three rounds to the chest. Pap-pap-pap. He arched back but absorbed the blow like a champ.

"General," he called back to me, his eyes wild. "Hal, I don't know if I can cut through all the rest with half of them shooting at us!"

Once again, I yelled up to the old man, "HERE!"

Finally, Mr. Johnson seemed to understand (or more likely just thought, might as well)-- and he launched the RPG right at me, the smoke tongue flickering toward me at an amazing speed.

"General... what..?"

When it reached me-- and you have to time these things-- I was in full swing with my left leg, connected, and hit the live grenade into the middle of the advancing black-clad pack.

BOOM!

Bits of rock and asshole flew in the air.

Chubbs looked at me and I said: "That's gotta be a double, for sure."

Two were coming up to Chubbs' left and I yelled, "Again! HERE!"

Then to Chubbs I said: "This looks like a base hit, left of the shortstop."

Fwwwwwwt!

Thwop-- BOOM!

My friend cheered, "And the crowd goes wild, bitches!" And knowing my rodeo-clown-turned-Near-Zombie-warrior friend, I'd shown him all he needed to know.

"Johnson," he called out and raised both of his Octx high into the air, red metal sheets, covered in the blood of past victims. He filled his chest with air and called out: "HERE!"

The eldest Swordsman nodded and even from more than a hundred yards away, I could see the off-white of his grin.

He yelled at the top of his lungs: "Tea-baggin' Helen Mirren!"

And it began.

Over the next two minutes, Mr. Johnson fired nearly every weapon in his arsenal. Anything that exploded, he launched down to Chubbs, and Chubbs reflected it back with a swipe of an Octx toward the on-coming advance.

A group approaching his left-- boom!

Seven advancing on the docks toward Karla's friends--boom!

The stone walls of CDC's secret loading dock rang with concussive boom! boom! boom! boom! until the agents who'd not been blown to bits had quickly fled out into the street.

TEN MINUTES LATER WE regrouped with Karla and her Ladies down at the truck docks.

A couple semis had gotten out-- but her group had disabled the remaining three. That was a big win in my book.

Me, I wasn't privy to the battle they'd fought-- I'm sure they'd been great but we'd had our own to barely escape. And once Chubbs and I drew half the agents' fire, she and her crew had taken out more than a dozen of the black-suited assholes themselves.

As we walked up, Karla said, "You guys make good targets," She chuckled and added: "Thanks for that."

"Everybody's gotta be good at something," I said, trying to act cool, because this girl was beautiful. What had Sun Tz--?

"And, you, wow," she said as Chubbs got to the top of a short set of stairs. "Baby, that was the sexiest thing I've seen--"

"What? Me?" He said but stopped when Karla had planted a big wet kiss on his mouth. When he tried to speak again, she silenced him with another.

"You're amazing, my Chubby-man."

I offered, simply to set the record straight: "The reflecting thing with, you know, the explosives coming down and bling! shooting them back, that was kinda my idea an--"

"Wait! Hold on..." Karla said when she finally broke away from molesting my Number Two man (Of course, she and the other Ladies had to stay aroused or crossover to FZ. Naturally, in that state, she would have a tendency toward sexual aggression. Chubbs, it seemed, had become the target and would have to, for the moment, endure those affections).

Exhausted, I slumped into a beaten up office chair, its wheels rattled as I slid sideways a couple feet. Next to me, two of the Ladies had collapsed into exhausted piles as well, and each put a heel on my armrest and pushed me back.

"Much obliged," I said and smiled.

"Anytime, General," one of them said, and we all laughed. I'm not sure how many had been with Karla but only four remained.

Each was dirtied, bloodied and inexplicably wearing a Russell Brand t-shirt to stay on the Near Zombie side.

I couldn't tell for sure, but it seemed they'd each worn different pictures of the actor. One I recognized as the movie poster for "Arthur," which in my book... trying to one-up Dudley Moore? Get over yourself.

Karla called again: "Hal! How did--"

"Jane Russell, sitting on my face, riding me like a ten-speed bike!"

"Hey, Mr. Johnson," I said as the old man climbed up a steel ladder on the far side of the dock and headed toward us.

He waved, tired.

One of the Ladies, the red-haired one, said: "Can someone please get him dosed, so I don't have to hear that nasty man say shit like that anymore?"

We hadn't yet told them that my supply had gone up with the grenades. But, it was time.

"Listen, we--"

"Hal!" Karla said yet again. "How the hell..?"

"What?"

She pointed down at my midsection, which as I've said, not a fan of being ogled, despite how pretty she was and--

"Your leg," she said. "How did that happen?"

One of the other Ladies leaned up from her resting spot on a busted-up pleather office couch and asked, "How did what happen?"

Chubbs laughed, "Weird huh?"

Karla nodded, "Yeah. I saw it get blown off."

"Right."

"Then how the hell do you have two legs, again?"

IN TRUTH, THAT ONE was a bit of a mystery to me, too, at that point.

But once I'd dispensed with a couple of agents and Chubbs had brilliantly taken over the fight, to be honest, I didn't have much left in me and collapsed to the dirt.

Sitting, leaning, I watched my friend do what he was born to do.

And then, the strangest thing.

My leg, sliced clean by shelving that had been launched with the grenade blast, was in the dirt just a few inches away from me-- useless to me now, I'd tossed it to the ground.

But what intrigued me as I looked down, I saw where it had been.

And at the cut, only flesh and nothing below, from the tear-line of my jeans, I saw what looked like tendrils. My best guess at the time, they were, incredibly, short bits of veins and sinew and tendon and strands of muscle... and all were slowly fluttering.

Almost reaching out.

Reaching out for what was just out of reach: my leg.

With the blasts ringing around me-- and the enemy rightfully having lost interest me-- I was tired, but slowly shifted my weight and moved closer to it.

"AND IT, WHAT, REATTACHED?" Karla said, her mouth hanging open.

I kicked both my legs in the air, crossed them and put them back down on the cement dock below me.

"Yep."

A low whoa! bubbled over our group-- which now numbered eight.

"How? How does that work?"

"I don't know," I said laughing. "But I think if we can find Chubbs' hands out there-- if they weren't eaten-- we could get them working again."

Karla looked to my friend and smiled, and moved back closer to him.

Then he said, dead serious: "Why would I do that?"

"Ha, ha!" She said, did a little hop, wrapped her arms around his neck and kissed him again, tenderly this time on the cheek.

This would have probably been a good time for introductions all around, but we were in a vulnerable spot and needed to get somewhere hidden, share what we all new, and come up with a plan to take Project Darwin down entirely.

"Okay, listen, is there anywhere nearby that, we…"

My voice faded as I stared out the dock bay doors.

It was nightfall and the lights behind us barely dim enough to see each other. But something, just outside the door, had rolled into view.

Then another.

And another.

The ginger-haired woman said, "Oh no."

Another said: "That… It couldn't be?" Then, creeping from her seat, keeping low but standing, she turned toward the woman near Chubbs. "Karla, is that what I think it is?"

Karla's yellowed NZ eyes were wide, and she shook her head slowly.

She took a step away from Chubbs, trying to get a better look.

He glanced at her, as I did, waiting for some idea of what these things were.

"Well," I said, standing. "Should we be running for our lives again or what?"

Chubbs added: "What are those? They're gimps or something, right?"

Karla looked around, her movements quicker now, and she nodded.

"No, not quite zombies," she said, putting her hand to her mouth. "But, sure, similar. Except these are what we've been calling 'blanks'"

At the word, two of the other Ladies popped out of their resting places and clustered with the group.

Just judging by their reaction-- they'd bravely faced the armed WWF agents minutes earlier, but this?

This was going to be really, really bad.

In front of us in a small splash of light, three of these "blank" gimps move toward each other and then, incredibly, they ran.

"What the..?"

And, just on the other side of the dock's concrete lip, I watched the three blanks combine. I blinked to see clearer as each pressed into the others, creating a mass of writhing flesh and veins, growing in size.

It looked familiar...

Then, I recalled it.

The geezer gimps in the old people's home. They'd done something similar, but not quite like this.

These creatures were as one, a bubbling mass, forming into what I did not know.

Karla said, "We gotta get outta here!"

"Not going that way."

"Back up and out. The entry way up top!"

"Why not--"

"Let's just go!"

Chubbs growled, clanked his Octx: "We can take that, whatever the hell it is!"

Karla put a tender hand on his face and said: "That's part of the problem. We don't know what it'll be yet."

"Meaning?"

"It's three times the size of any of us, and it could become anything."

Chubbs looked to me and Mr. Johnson who was fiddling with his pocket, but his face was the same shade of terror as the rest of us.

"What do you mean 'anything'?"

Then, two more appeared, smashed into it.

Then another.

And another.

Blanks were racing in but not at us; each was ramming its flesh into the growing mass. It grew each time another--

Two more.

Then four more.

"Oh, Christ, this is bad!"

"Karla, what is that thing?"

The Ginger woman had grabbed Mr. Johnson and two other Ladies, they were starting the climb. She called to us: "Come on!"

Karla hesitated. Her eyes on the blob of writhing flesh and muscle and soft bones, she said:

"It can be anything. They can be anything. They can combine or, sometimes it's just a couple of them taking different forms," she said, taking a step forward. "One is a wolf. One morphs into a bear or even a feral pig."

"What? A pig?"

"Deadly, Chubbs." She said, her eyes damp and red. "Teeth, fangs and claws. They can become anything, but I've never seen... so many."

I walked next to her, looked over at the rest of our group, yelling at them to move faster. As it grew, I could feel its evil. I could feel it deep into my bones.

"Maybe we can take out the leader here," I said, my breath turning a bit raspy. "Which one--?"

"No," Karla's voice raised as the creature in front of us began to form. Still, blanks were smashing into it, one after another. "They're all blanks. Don't you get that?"

Chubbs was up on the balls of his feet, ready for nearly anything.

"Then how are they..." My voice trailed off. I knew what she was about to say but still didn't understand it. She'd mentioned it earlier, when we'd first come into the CDC.

"The First Patron," she said and swallowed hard. The mass of blank gimps was taking form. "He... or she... it's not even human anymore. It's been pushed way past that. It's powerful now. It created the blanks, and it controls them."

"To do what? What's it going--?"

Before us, the mass lifted itself, easily thirty feet high, twisted onto and within itself. A shrieking sound erupted and we stood, frozen by fear.

It growled and churned and spun, then again-- a shriek but fuller and deeper now.

Quietly, I could hear Karla saying, "Go. We can't... we--"

In a slap of light and energy that put us flat on our backs, it took form.

Regaining my footing, I made it up to my elbows first and tried to decipher what I was seeing. It was--

"A dragon??? "

"We... we should have run the first moment we saw it," Karla mumbled, looking side to side.

I turned to her: "You said lions and tigers and bears and shit!"

The storybook lizard, three stories high, lifted up onto its powerful back haunches, and roared so loud, so fiercely, our people climbing the far wall stopped and covered their heads.

"Dragons aren't real!" I yelled, my eyes on Karla because in truth I couldn't look at it. "They're not re--"

"The First Patron willed it to be a dragon, so it's a fucking dragon, Hal!"

The lizard-like skin rippled as the massive creature spread its wings, and its eyes seemed to light from behind.

"What can--?"

Then, it spit a column of fire toward our friends at the wall.

"No!"

Mr. Johnson and the others had crouched behind a stack of boulders and when the flame hit, part of the stack incinerated.

They screamed.

Finally, I looked back at it.

Huge, all teeth and claws. It was a living nightmare.

Karla yelled, "It's nearly at full manifest. Once it's complete, there'll be nothing we can do--"

"HEY!"

My head snapped toward the group at the wall, but it hadn't been them calling out. They were huddling close, waiting for the next blast.

Then I realized it.

"Where's..?"

"HEY, I'm talking at you!"

Down, at the edge of the ramp, Chubbs was waving his Octx at the giant, writhing creature.

"You're like Harry Potter's wet dream or something?" He yelled at it, finally getting its attention. "What a friggin' joke you are!"

The dragon moved toward Chubbs and I yelled at the group: "Move, move!"

Karla began to step toward Chubbs, but he turned and looked at her, then a sweet smile crossed his lips.

I'd seen him smile a hundred times. It's what the guy did.

But this one? Not like this. This one was special. This was a smile, I think, he'd kept to himself a long, long time.

It had only been minutes between the two of them, Karla and him. But this was a smile he'd saved, maybe his entire life.

This was the one he'd kept until now, so he could give it to the woman who'd stolen his heart.

He said to her, "Wait, Karla."

She hesitated, and looked up. The creature took another step forward. She shook her head: "Chubbs, no. We can all--"

He gave her the smile again, looked sideways at her and held up one of his red hands: Stop.

The dragon hadn't refueled its flame but wasn't going to rely on that. It took a swipe at Chubbs, but he was too quick, rolled to the side.

"Chubbs!"

Another swipe, the ex-rodeo clown up on the balls of the feet, he slipped away from that, too.

The creature's deafening snarls filled the cavern. The sound of its roaring, its claws scraping at concrete was too loud...but I knew he was singing to himself that damn song.

And if he could have heard my thoughts at that moment, he'd have heard this: sing, man, sing.

The dragon furious, roared again, lifted both claws and plunged its jaws, eyes blazing bright, down at Chubbs, its huge teeth clamping into the concrete.

My friend was no longer in sight.

"No," I whispered. "I don't believe it. He'll..."

"Chubbs!"

The dragon, blinked, twisted its head as it tried to free itself. Its teeth had sunk so deep into the concrete, it was stuck for the moment.

Its hind legs pulled and shifted.

I looked up and cheered-- the group had made it to the entrance!

Chubbs had done it, but... wait!

Then, we saw him!

Moments before the dragon freed itself, he slashed with his Octx at its thick, scaly cheek and slipped through the breach.

"All right!" I yelled, then: "Come on! Let's get outta here, man!"

Chubbs looked toward me and then Karla, but he knew like we did. Once the dragon was freed, we were all done.

All three of us.

So, I believe he felt he'd made the only decision he could.

He stuck at the dragon, slicing into the neck. Then his other Octx, a little higher. The first came out, cutting into its flesh a little higher as he climbed up the beast's skull.

"No, no, no!"

In the moment before the creature freed its head, Chubbs was sitting behind its head, Octx dug in deep as they could go.

It roared again, screeching terribly, trying to shake him off. But Chubbs wasn't going to be shaken off. He was going to ride it as long as he had to.

Just like those he used to protect, those years ago. Ride it out.

The creature was up on its back legs again, swiping at him, trying to claw him off its neck, but couldn't, the pain of the Octx slicing into its flesh driving it mad, it took off fast running out of sight.

Karla and I stood there.

All that was left was its roar, the thumping of its feet.

As it got farther and farther away.

There were tears in her eyes when she turned to me.

"Maybe… maybe he can jump off and--"

I shook my head. He's going to ride it out, I thought. Jumping off would only be serving himself up as an easy target.

Overcome with my own sadness, he was my best friend in this fucked up undead world. But, my heart lightened a little when I remembered what Mr. Johnson had said about him earlier that day--

 Ain't nothing sadder than a clown with no rodeo.

Chubbs, at last, had found it.

KARLA EXPLAINED TO ME how the head of the WWF attack force, the one I'd seen in the cart, had slipped away.

They weren't out of the picture yet-- not at all.

But that wasn't our biggest problem, the most dangerous threat.

Before this was over, we'd have to take out the First Patron.

And as Karla explained to me what exactly this creature was-- and what it was capable of-- I thought, after Chubbs' sacrifice, we had to take it on.

But without him?

"We don't have an army, Hal. And we don't have time to build one up. There's just a handful of us. It's impossible, isn't it?"

"Ah. When has that ever stopped us?"

"Uh, well, I've only been at this for a couple--"

"Yeah, same here. Just a day or so."

"So, it's not like there's some long, storied history of beating impossible odds or--"

"No, no. I get it, but it, you know, the sentiment is the same."

"Right. Got it. So, we're dead, right?"

"Yeah, probably."

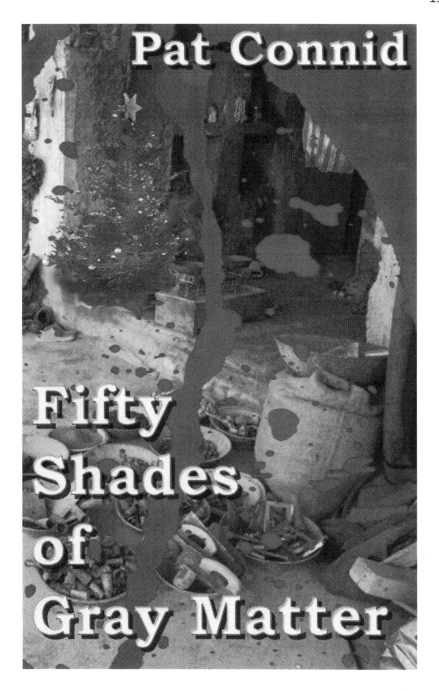

BOOK FIVE

"This keeps up, and I think 1983 will be The Year of Clay Savage!"

Those words were spoken by one Mr. Clay Eliot Savage on May 10th, 1983.

Two things are, of course, immediately apparent from that particular statement.

First, Clay Savage was the sort of man who would speak of himself in the third person.

Second, that particular declaration would go down as The Third Most Inaccurate Statement of 1983*.

*Footnote: It was narrowly beat out by The Second Most Inaccurate Statement of 1983, which was of course awarded to an utterance during a private affair, in the early morning hours of February 27th in a filmmaker's coastal hideaway: "No, no. I think the Ewoks will be a fan-favorite and don't, actually, darken the movie's legacy a single bit."

The 37 year-old copyeditor had voiced previously how he'd felt the year had been a little "touch-and-go" at the start (Clay was someone who would frequently voice an entry in his own life's scorecard or prognosticate about likely future conditions, as if he were a natural force like the weather. Or pork belly futures).

This revised, optimistic forecast had been inspired by what was supposed to be a routine, bi-yearly visit to his primary care physician earlier that afternoon.

He'd been declared in very good health for "a man of his age." Just after the doctor had completed the compulsory fly-by visit (to justify the higher rate on the insurance company's fee schedule), the older gentleman stopped at the door. He turned back, gave Clay a hard stare and sighed.

"Please stop playing with the blood pressure cuff, Mr. Savage."

"Oh, sorry," Clay said, eyes sparkling slightly. "It just kinda makes my fingers all tingly when it gets tight."

"Yes, but--"

"I wonder what else I can wrap it around?"

"Please, Mr. Savage," Dr. Mattingly said and snatched the cuff from his patient's fingers. He'd just about left without another word when a thought struck him. "Listen, I don't know if you'd be interested but--"

He then hesitated.

Was it unethical to refer to a perfectly healthy (comparatively speaking) patient? Would it be considered immoral to refer the man with the unfortunate, fat mustache to the study group?

Realizing it might, the doctor turned and closed the door.

"Mr. Savage, that sort of thing, with the cuff-- no, no. Please leave it," he said, forcing a smile. "You know, there are those not quite... as healthy as yourself."

"Yes, Clay Savage works in the news business, sir," he said, nodding, eyes hooded. The little man tugged on the edges of his mustache. "You should see the shit that crosses my desk."

"I'm sure, and--"

"It'd make your hair turn white."

The doctor rubbed his bald head and decided, yes, Clay Savage would make a fine candidate.

"Clay, there is a clinical trial going on right now for a, uh, forward-looking narcolepsy medicine."

"Clinical trial? Ah yes," Clay said, petting his lip creature as an evil villain may stroke a fat, white Persian (or, possibly, a cat). "Cutting edge medicine. We live in an era of wonders, doctor! Clay Savage always says if you are not constantly amazed by this great big blue marble we call 'the world,' you ain't paying attention!"

The doctor forced a laugh and stood.

"Well, if you're interested, I can give you the number to the study group. Right here in town. You do a couple tests, and you get to be a part of, well, shaping the future."

"Really." Another tug at the thick hair above the man's lip. "But I don't actually have narcolepsy." He then added earnestly, "Is that a problem?"

"Not an issue," the doctor said and lowered his voice by a degree. "You get tired, don't you?"

"Sure."

"It's just like that."

"Okay."

"And," the man in the white lab coat said, stuffing his hands into its pockets. "You're compensated seventeen-hundred dollars for the testing time, overnight stays, that sort of thing."

"Really?"

The doctor leaned toward the counter, slipping a business card from his pocket and started to write a telephone number on it. He then thought better of it, tore it up, tossed it out and instead pulled a post-it note from a cheery little plastic case (a premium dropped-off courtesy of a manufacturer of abdominal stents).

A moment later, he handed the telephone number to Clay who took it and held it as if it were a check from Publisher's Clearing House.

"Oh, I could--" Clay closed his eyes for a moment, then said. "I've always wanted to travel."

"Then there's your ticket, Clay! Wonderful."

"Oooo... maybe Spain! Have you ever been to Spain?"

"No, never been," the doctor said and turned the knob, then grinned. "But, they say the ladies are insane there."

"Oh," the seated man said and picked something white out of his facial hair. "If there's some sort of mental health issue there--"

"No, no. It was, you know, the song..."

"Hey, I've always wanted a new car! That's what I'll do with it. Clay Savage has always driven used. Chevys, Volvos, Datsuns..."

The doctor furrowed his brow.

"That, well, seventeen-hundred dollars won't really buy you a new car, though, Mr. Savage."

His excitement dimmed, momentarily, until the paunchy copyeditor suddenly had a thought, a possible solution for this troubling new-car-less quandary.

"I wonder if there are other clinical trials that, you know, pay people."

"SO, HE'D DONE IT to himself?"

Karla looked at me and nodded slowly.

She'd broken down, crying, after Chubbs had been carried off. It seemed like it might have been the first time she'd let go like that in a while, so I'd sat with her quietly on a long, busted up filing cabinet lying on its side.

Mr. Johnson and the Ladies had already made it back into the main CDC complex. We were going to head up the moment she was ready.

Until then, she told me what she knew about the First Patron.

"Trust me there are dozens, if not hundreds, that were complicit," she said. "He wasn't, you know, sick. So, the perfect subject to test new medicines on."

"Ugh!"

"Lotions and potions, pills, salves, oils and ointments. All of this, basically in secret, too, as provided by non-disclosure agreements-- he'd been signed up as guinea pig for drugs to treat eczema, hair loss, yellow teeth, bad breath, heartburn, water-on-the-knee, planters warts--"

"Eeewwww!"

"There probably isn't a single drug in the last three decades-- approved, unapproved or even eventually deemed unfit for public consumption-- that hadn't coursed through his veins at some point."

We had to get moving, it was unsafe standing there at the truck bays of the CDC. But, with what seemed to be ahead of us, another moment's rest wouldn't kill us (I hoped).

"What possesses a guy to do that? Allow that to happen to him?"

"I think he just liked all the... attention," she said. "He said as a kid, he didn't have a lot of friends. And when it came to group activities, like kickball, he didn't just get picked last; he didn't get picked at all."

"Wow, sad."

"The kids booted him off the local Dungeons & Dragons chapter because he'd freak out every time he saw the box," she said, stretching her arms. "Later, he once even put a Save the Wales bumper sticker on his car. That night a small go-team from Greenpeace snuck over and scraped it off."

"Sucks."

"Yeah."

"So, this started out because he signed up to get injected with all that stuff because he's lonely?" It made me feel a little sorry for him. Then I remembered he'd created the creature that had taken my friend. Not so sorry. "So, what does all that goop do to you? All those chemicals?"

Karla frowned, then shrugged.

She knew more than she was telling me.

Standing slowly, she checked her twin, modified rifles to be sure they were still secured. And loaded.

For being reduced in size, I'd have thought the small AK-47 magazines would have run low quickly. I wasn't sure where she was keeping her backup ammunition. I had some ideas, most of which were arguably impractical (and would require exceptional muscle control and pre-conditioning which would likely entail a rather disciplined schedule of special, personally tailored exercises).

Most likely, she kept spares clips in the pack secured to the small of her back (although, I hadn't discounted the other possibilities outright).

I pressed: "All that messing with your body? Your DNA, RNA... TNA. Is that a thing?"

"No."

"Whatever," I said. "Crazy."

She raised an eyebrow and said, "This coming from the guy who pops ED medicine like Skittles so that he can keep a 24-7 hard on."

"Steady on," I said. "Apples and Oranges! I'm trying to Save All of Mankind--"

"--With a Boner," she said and smiled.

Sure, it was true.

Only the night before, I'd tried to kill myself after being infected with the ZBF (zombie bird flu). But instead of over-dosing on pain meds, I'd popped a bunch of Erectile Dysfunction pills.

With that tiny bit of blood diverted from my brain, I now keep in a Near-Zombie, NZ, state.

Chubbs had been the first to join my quest to rid the world of the undead (if nothing but to clear up the interstates) and our octogenarian-plus Mr. Johnson was number three.

Yes, we are the ones you've heard of.

We are the turgid.
We are The Swordsmen.
And, we were down by one.

WE CLIMBED BACK UP the rounded walls of the cavernous, hidden loading bays of the CDC. Only minutes earlier, we'd scaled down this way to battle back the WWF agents who'd pinned down Karla's team.

Not surprisingly, going up was even harder to manage.

As we climbed over the uneven incline of dirt, rock and office furniture, heading for the passage to take us back into the CDC complex, I followed her lead.

She was dressed both fashionably and combat-ready. Mostly thick leather, except for the Russell Brand t-shirt her entire team wore (inexplicably, their version of our ED regimen). Thinking back now, I knew very little about Karla at that time.

But I felt I could trust her. Still, something nagged at me that she knew a lot more than she'd so far let on.

"So, the First Patron and WWF, they're working together?"

"No, can't be. I've seen WWF agents ripped to shreds by the things the First Patron has turned his blanks into. Tigers and wild dogs. Emus with crocodile jaws."

"Jeesus!" I said, stumbling on a broken pencil sharpener momentarily. "How does he… or it… do that?"

"He's no longer entirely human," she said and her voice sounded hollow. "The combinations of the various types of chemicals over the years has withered his body but swelled his brain. Huge. Then synapses and new pathways grew."

"Give me a break. So now he's telekinetic?"

"Yeah, what a stretch," she said, getting a bit ahead of me. "Undead zombies roam the earth and the WWF is developing a serum to revert man to caveman. But ESP? That's freaky!"

"Well, in that context..."

"But, no actually," she continued. "He's had so many wires plugged into him. Leads and chips, implanted under the skin. At one point, you know how some people get piercings? This guy gets electronic couplings with brass contacts instead!"

"Kids today."

"Well, with all that data flowing out, I don't know, maybe one of the drugs, or a combo of them, but it seems his brain created neural pathways out to the monitoring stations."

"What?"

"Yeah, then megabytes of data becomes gigabytes, terabytes-- he learns to send commands into our computers. They tried to shut it down once he could take them over, but by that time..."

"Too late."

"No, we'd run over budget."

"Oh."

"And by the next quarter, when we could contract the IT guys to disconnect him, he'd become a part of it. Too strong. Couldn't stop him at that point."

"That's terrifying."

"But, you've seen it. You've seen what he can do."

I had seen it.

Before my eyes, dozens of gimps, "blanks" controlled by the First Patron had mashed together and formed into a bloody dragon, for God's sake. My second-in-command, Chubbs had taken it on by himself-- and was dragged away.

We'd been spared death-by-dragon, but without his meds-- even if he survived the thing-- Chubbs would be full-zombie any time now. Our supply had blown up but before that, earlier, I'd slipped a couple pills into Mr. Johnson's shirt pocket-- I had taken one of those, Chubbs hadn't.

We'd reached a lip in the rock and dirt, which served as a landing area by this door of the giant chamber.

I hadn't realized we'd gotten there already. She'd taken that last step upward and spun back toward me.

"Hey," she said. "Are you--?" she said, just a few paces in front of me. We'd been climbing up, so actually she was ahead and up about two or three feet. So, I'm not trying to be Hal, the Swordsman Zombie-Slaying Perv, but if I had this view (especially wrapped in the shiny leather) I could probably climb a little farther.

Like, oh, Everest.

"Nope, what did you see? Something up there seemed to get your attention, just a moment ago," I said quickly, finding a spot to look at on a nearby wall.

"Uh huh."

She stepped into the dark passage-- darker than I remember it-- but surprised me when she quickly returned before I could even take my last step onto the ground in front of the door.

"What are you--?"

She interrupted me, "Is this..?", but didn't even bother to wait for an answer, whipping past me along the wall. When she looked back, her face had drained of blood.

"What's up?"

She scowled at me, and wrapped her leather clad fingers around each hip.

"Oh, my god..."

"What?" I said, getting a little panicked. Walking forward, I traced her route back to the dark passage leading into the CDC.

What had she seen?

A dead body?

A gimp, hiding in the dark?

Actually, those I could handle.

But, jeez, no spiders! Fuck no (and that's not a fear, it's a phobia, totally different thing and very, very serious. Like a medical condition. Linked to incontinence, jitters and even shrieking, momentary crying jags. Look it up).

"Is it... hairy?"

"What??" Karla blew past me, into the dark passage, then I heard a repetitive thud as she banged her fist against rock. "Collapsed. It's blocked."

"Oh, whew."

"What, 'whew'? I want to know if my Ladies made it through okay," she said, frowning at me.

From deeper in the passage, I heard a voice: "Hello?" And, again, more muffled?

Then, "General, that you?"

I pointed: "See, that 'whew,' they're okay," I said. Then to Mr. Johnson, I shouted through the rock: "You guys okay, right?"

It took a moment-- like old-timey long distance calling, via ocean cable. You had to wait for an answer back.

"Yep. Me and the Ladies made it through but when Chubbs was fighting that big lizard thing, all that ruckus loosened up the rock. Came down just as we were sittin' here waiting for you guys."

Karla looked down at her hands and turned away.

"Okay," I said to the world's only other Swordsman now. "Why don't you guys head up and meet us down here at the trucking docks? Take the Rascal®."

I heard Karla chuckle softly to herself.

"Jeez, you guys are a mess."

"It's a very powerful Rascal®, actually."

"I'm sure it is."

"What's the plan then, General?" Johnson shouted, his voice already getting a bit hoarse. "We going after those trucks that got away with the gimp virus?"

Ah yes. A plan. I knew I was missing something.

"Let's work it out when we regroup," I yelled through the fallen rock and jerked a thumb toward the way we'd come. Karla nodded. "See you in a few."

After a rich and enlightening chat on the way up, we instead walked most of the way back in silence.

I'd also noticed she'd had me take the lead down. Hmm. Probably so I could defend from the front, if necessary.

"Well, I know you've got your super old-guy scooter but if we're going anywhere, we should try and get one of these trucks up and moving."

Two had been able to get on the road before we stopped them, so there were the burnt-out remains of three big trucks in the bay-- Karla herself had bombed out these while her Ladies were busy with the WWF agents.

"If any of them are salvageable, it'll be the one at the far end," she said and pointed. "I'd torched these two but only had enough explosives left to take out the trailer in that last one."

Looking at it more closely, she was right: the twenty-five foot container had been blasted out of shape, but the cab seemed okay.

They'd been loaded, naturally, with their trailers closest to the truck bay. So, the trick would be simply unhooking the cab from the trailer and, if we could get it started, we'd be set.

However, I didn't know much about making that happen.

First, though, we'd have to get if free from its burnt up haul. I jumped down next to the still-smoking trailer, searching underneath for some sort of hitch.

Karla stayed up top, and watched for any baddies that might approach.

Finally, it took a few minutes, I'd pulled out enough charred bits of boxes, metal and even human fleshy bits until I could get my hands near the collar that seemed to keep both together.

"Is there..." I said, calling up, "Some sort of hydraulics that holds this in place? Like a release in the cab?"

"Dunno," Karla said, walking over, her boots scraping against the sand above me. "Trucks aren't my..."

Her voice trailed off. That seemed odd, so I took a moment to catch my breath and looked up.

"Hal?"

She'd been in a bit of a daze since the trip back down. Now, her voice was sharp again. And, again, there was something in it I didn't like.

"Hal?" She repeated. "What's that? By your foot? What are...?"

By now, you'd have thought the sight of a dead body wouldn't have affected her. But this did. It didn't make sense.

"It's, I dunno," I said, shrugging. "A torso. It's a wom--" This, I thought, was one of her crew. One that hadn't been so lucky. Damn.

Grabbing some black plastic, I moved to cover the remains up. But she stopped me and insisted I turn the girl over.

"Karla..."

"Hal, do it!"

Reaching down, I gently grabbed the shoulder of the dead woman and tried to turn her from back to front.

Wedged a little, it took a moment. Then the body finally flipped over, with a wet, smacking sound. Above me, I heard her suck in a quick breath.

Karla said: "Oh, sweet Jesus..."

MR. JOHNSON KNEW HIS way back toward the hidden ramp, the one surrounded by the evergreens on the outside, after having earlier made a complete tour of the lower, secret catacombs of the CDC main complex.

This was better than earlier, when he'd wandered the lower level by himself.

This time, given the company, he wouldn't have complained, had you asked him.

"I can't complain," he said walking along side two of the Ladies, one on either side of him.

It had been a few years since he'd been around a couple of pretty young girls.

"It's been a few years since I've been around--"

Okay, stop it now, will you? Seriously.

Johnson stared upward and said, "My ball still hasn't dropped, you know that?"

The dark-haired young woman next to him wrapped her small arms around his right sinewy bicep.

"What?" She laughed and shook her head. "You say such odd things."

"Never mind," Johnson said and the grumpiness was quickly gone. A smile pulled to his lips.

Initially, he'd been worried after Hal and he had gotten separated, once again. But, with such lovely company...

There were just a couple more turns until they'd be back to the ramp door. Then up top into the parking lot from where the three Swordsmen had come earlier.

"It's just up here," he said, the euphoria of battle won still tingling his skin. "Two more lefts."

"What is?"

"The... well, the door to the lot, of course," he said and shrugged. "We'll grab the Rascal®, but I'm gonna have to get strategic to get you four Ladies on there."

The young woman holding his arm laughed.

"We'll manage, I'm sure," the Ginger Lady to his left said. "So, it's just us?"
Johnson found himself getting a little fatigued-- previously, his nights had been TV and board games. His days, often, napping through the heat.

So, all this running around and climbing (not to mention the explosives and the killing) was taking it out of him. A little. Just a little.

The smile grew a little bit, and then he remembered the red-haired girl had asked him a question.

"Well, yeah, there's... what do you mean?"

He slowed but the woman at his arm pushed forward, keeping their pace.

One of the Ladies had gone twenty feet ahead, on point.

Another was behind, he glanced back to her, and she answered his question.

"Don't you Swordsmen have other recruits?"

The old man laughed.

"Well, no, we just..."

His words fell short, as he watched the pretty, young girl in front of them stumble a little. She seemed to be having trouble with her shoes, but no, found her footing--

Again. It was like she was tripping over something, catching herself.

"Hey, darlin' are you all--"

"She's fine," said the Ginger Lady holding his arm.

Sure, he thought. They were all tired. In fact he was surprised he had...

"When did you..." Mr. Johnson looked toward the red-haired woman. To his left, the young girl with the funny giggles was now walking.

"When did you guys trade... you know... places? I thought she..."

"WHAT IS IT, KARLA? Say something, goddamn it!"

She looked shell-shocked and for the moment, couldn't find any words.

I crouched down and looked closer at the body near my feet. She'd asked me to turn the dead girl over only moments earlier. I thought she'd been upset at the sight of her dead friend.

That wasn't it.

Karla was dazed, lost in some sort of panic-fog. I yelled my question again.

Her glassy eyes looked at me but didn't seem to focus. At least, not entirely.

"It's… I don't understand," she said and rubbed her temples. "How… did..?"

Then it hit me.

I recognized her.

I knew this girl.

"Hold on," I said backing up a step, then went down to one knee. "Is that..? Is that your red-haired crewmember?"

Karla nodded and squeezed her eyes shut.

"How… I mean," I said, moved in and softly pushed a strand of hair away from her face. It was heavy, sticky with drying blood. "But, I was just talking to--"

I jumped up, now my mind was whirring, my eyes locked on the corpse at my feet.

Another glance at Karla, then I looked at the far wall, where we'd originally come down into the CDC's cavernous, secret loading docks.

Where Johnson had gone through with the remaining four Ladies.

Then, I jumped up back onto the deck of the truck bay.

And ran.

As fast as I could.

Climbing, tripping, grabbing at the ropes, I raced toward the opening that only minutes earlier we'd seen blocked.

It didn't matter. Somehow, I had to warn him.

JOHNSON'S ELATION FADED AND while real concern had not yet set in, confusion certainly had.

Strangely, the woman at his arm, she looked... different. And, the noises...

"Ooof, ungn..."

His head snapped forward and saw the first woman not just stumbling but now trembling, shaking. Then she dropped her weapon, but it seemed to just turn to air!

"What in the fuc-- hey," he said to the Ginger Lady next to him. "Not so hard, now. Don't forget I'm old and bits--"

He stopped talking as the woman behind him called out saying, "Dammit, too far. Gah-gn--- getting out of range."

Johnson's confusion only doubled.

It hadn't even made sense, what she said.

"Now, we've got, hey--!"

The red-haired beauty next to him was now also twitching, then shaking, then convulsing!

Fear gripped his throat as he watched, as she tugged and pulled at his arm, as she struggled to... whatever she was doing.

"Hellfire, girl, do I need to stuff a wallet in your mouth or sumthin', so's you don't bite off your tongue, or--"

Strangely, he'd seen it before he'd heard the wet snap and tear.

The Ginger Lady took a few steps back the way they'd come and stopped shaking.

She was smiling now.

Still holding Mr. Johnson's arm.

But, this time, she was standing a few feet away from him after pulling it off his body.

RACING, SCRAMBLING TO THE top of the wall, I was choking back the anger, swallowing my fear.

"Johnson!" I yelled, then screamed as loud as I could: "Johnson!"

Moments away from losing the only other Swordsman left, I knew there was nothing for me to do-- even if I got to the top in time, he'd never hear me through the blockage in the passageway.

From deep inside the CDC, I heard his scream.

High pitched at first, then it was uncertain-- like a wordless question-- the shrill of his voice arched in volume, upward for only a second, then faded away.

All I could do was stand and stare at the dark hole at the ridge, just above me. Falling to my knees, I clenched my hands into white fists.

From below, Karla yelled up: "We have to go!"

Either with the help of the WWF agents or without their knowledge, the First Patron had taken the place of the remaining four Ladies. Had he killed them, one-by-one, as one of his slave gimps mirrored each's image, while another was hiding away the corpse?

All I knew was I'd lost both Chubbs and, now, Mr. Johnson to this bastard. The First Patron had used his zombie proxies to kill my only two friends left in the world.

Rage coursed through me, and I realized I was running only when my breaths began to sound like growls.

And, as I came back down to Karla at the dirty, dusty and bloody cement pad of the loading docks, I had one thought at the top of my mind:

"No more games, Karla. What aren't you telling me?"

The ground shook beneath us. Somewhere deep.

"We need to get out of the open here," she said. Her eyes traced the huge cavernous area, then she started heading toward the far wall-- away from where I'd come. "If the First Patron can reach all the way up there, toward the ramp, we're sitting ducks here."

"Why is he attacking us? How are we a threat?"

She began running when the next rumbling hit, and I followed closely behind her-- I didn't trust her, but she was the only one left on my side.

If she was on my side.

I asked again, "Why is he attacking us?"

She didn't answer. That is, she didn't say anything. I grabbed her arm and spun her back toward me.

Her face told me everything.

"He's after you," I said and got only silence back. "Isn't he?"

A dull explosion rocked deep beneath our feet, this wasn't just a tremor. She spun to bolt but I held her.

Her eyes were wild as bits of grit fell onto us. Small pebbles tink-tink-tinked against the metal plate on the lip of the truck bay.

The panic on her face turned to anger and her hands moved for the rifles strapped to her chest. I didn't even try to stop her.

I only said, "Really?"

She looked at me, then the anger melted away.

Another rumble beneath us, but she just nodded to herself.

"You probably already worked it out. I'm so-- I'm sorry."

"Sure, of course," I said to her. "But, you know, you should say it... that part. The stuff you know that I've worked out."

"I-- I can't."

"Listen," I said. "He's coming, Karla! So you know I know most of what you need to tell me so just, you know, say it." Maybe it was paranoia, but it did feel like something was coming. But, I needed to know. "Just go ahead. Right, I know because I did work it out, but it's more, you know, cleansing if you just say it," I said. "Beside, you owe me that."

Nodding again, but slower, she took a deep breath.

"Yeah," she said. "I was just a part of the team--"

"Christ, you were on the medical team. You gave him--"

"No," she said quickly. "I never administered drugs to him. Any of it. But we did his physicals, monitored his well-being."

It took me a moment to pick it up.

Something was flapping around outside the truck bay doors. Softly, like large, damp moth wings. Then it grew louder.

Karla cocked her head, she'd heard it.

I said: "Okay, run now."

We were sprinting toward the far wall-- there was an indentation I hadn't noticed before.

I followed her down a short ladder, dropped to the concrete and we ran to a small door. She punched in a couple numbers and the door popped ajar. We shoved it open.

"Through here," she said. "He'll be sending more of those things, looking for us."

Before us was a short hallway with a small maintenance closet to the right, conference room on the left.

"I was second in charge," she said and flipped on the lights of the conference room. We closed the door behind us. "We took care of his living space and, eventually, isolated him from the world. Entirely."

There was a phone on the table. Out of habit, I tried it. Nothing.

"This isn't happening," she said.

"We can't stay here, Karla!"

"I can't believe... you know, when Clay, first came to us he was so, you know, harmless. I remember thinking that. Lived by himself in midtown. Real simple guy."

"He didn't have cats did he?" I asked, squinted my eyes. "Never did feel right about a guy that had cats."

"No, he didn't like animals, actually. He said they didn't get along."

I had the two spikes in my chest as weapons but very little juice left in my flame thrower. If anything confronted us like we'd seen before, no way I was winning that battle.

"Why is he after us? What threat are we to him?"

She said, Clay had begun to change into something different. He'd begun to call himself the First Patron and would only laugh when asked to explain what the silly title meant.

"Laugh at us," she said. "His entire demeanor had changed. He wasn't the shy, nervous Clay. It was almost... he acted like he was in charge now."

"See, me, I'm thinking that should set off red flags."

"But, still, it was all going so well. The data he was giving us was priceless, I was told." She stood up, checked inside a cabinet. Empty, she closed it. "But it had been a part of... the First Patron's plan. He'd discovered a way to control the data leaving his body. Then to manipulate how it... manifested."

"Karla..."

She cracked the door open, looking down the hall. She closed it again.

"With Project Darwin, the WWF was going to set mankind back by manipulating the genetic code," she said and walked back to the table. "Mankind 1.0, you could say."

"He hijacked their research."

"Exactly, and then inserted his own genetic material, that's why they all look the way they do. The gimps are a hybrid of WWF's Project Darwin and... Clay."

"And he can control them?"

"A limited range," she said and looked at me. "We'd put up a firewall between Clay's servers and the outside world."

"What if he gets through the firewall?"

This is what terrified her.

Her lips shook and she said, "Every undead gimp would be under his control. Eventually, he'd control armies of those things. Millions of them."

The room shook, the booms beneath us coming like contractions, shorter in between, more concussive each time.

"First Patron doesn't mean he's the first of their kind. It means he's the leader." The room shook, she grabbed the table. "The leader of a zombie army, growing every day. He's going to overthrow every government on the planet."

I stared at her hard.

"So, he needs the code to get through the firewall. To get his mind out, past these walls," I said.

She said nothing. Just stepped back, chewing her lip.

"Ah," I said. Sometimes it takes me a while, but usually I'll get there. But part of me wishes I hadn't. "And you have it. You have the code."

"Yes."

Such a powerful, simple word.

And it was as if that word had been the trigger to blast us into a realm of pure light and sound, and for just an instant we'd frozen in that moment, suspended in air, time and space.

She fell, but in the split second before she did (and I only remembered this a long time later), she shoved me with everything she had out the door of the conference room.

The fluorescent tubes above us exploded, the crystals of glass bursting through the air like tiny grains of starlight.

I was tumbling backwards, feet over head, into the hallway where the floor had not given way.

Another flash of light, but that had come from within my own skull, as my head banged off the carpeted concrete floor and I spun again, landing hard.

I looked up to the door of the conference room, as if peering into another world, like an alien observer witnessing something behind a protective membrane of flame and smoke.

Karla was slipping downward, flowing against the tide of the rest of the world-- and then she was gone, disappeared somewhere below me.

Everything was dark again, and having swallowed Karla, the ground below me was now hungry for me. I tried to get up and run but only got a few long steps until there was no more floor to step upon, falling, falling, it felt like every cell in my body was spinning in place.

A long drop.

Was I flying, not falling?

I landed hard (not flying: check). The impact had stolen my breath and my lungs were slow to recover it.

The dull rumbling continued, all around me, but began to fade as an odd dawn rose in front of me.

It was another room-- I'd fallen straight into the hall below. The glow was the emergency lights.

I entered.

The room was dark, but the air heavy with electricity.

Above me more than a dozen thick conduits, as large as sewer drains all led out of the room.

From their origin, behind me, I heard an unpleasant voice.

"And who might you be?

KARLA FOUGHT TO STAY on her feet but couldn't-- then simply fought to stay conscious.

She'd fallen into a large, cluttered room.

Then she recognized it as the cafeteria where she'd eaten hundreds of stale lunches. This seemed right-- she'd fallen hard onto a long lunch table, sending some used, dirty dishware to the floor.

No time to recover from the fall, though.

She wasn't alone in the room.

The only light was coming from above but going up that way wasn't possible.

And she'd seen, as she fell, what were just to her left-- not running that way.

Hopping down, she sprinted away from them but others were there, too, and she could feel their arms, fingers, slimy and shredded, reaching and grabbing for her.

"No!"

She broke free from the gimps and ran another way, but there were still more that way. From every direction they were moving toward her-- dozens and dozens of them. Then, it seemed, a hundred, maybe hundreds, all had been locked away in the room, as if the First Patron had gathered them there like some waiting undead battalion.

Another wall, only stacks upon stacks of chairs. It was all she had, she began to climb, uneasily up the stack.

Their groans grew louder as more and more picked up her scent. Fingers and hands, slimy and sloppy reached for her but couldn't hold. Panicked, she would climb a few feet, slip a little, and climb more.

This staggered progression, slathered with fear that she'd slip all the way to the bottom with every falter, she grunted and yelled, climbing higher and higher up the stacks of chairs.

"Let GO!" she screamed as they grew closer and clawed at her leg, one leaving a yellowed fingernail stuck in her skin.

At the top, she pushed at the ceiling above but it wouldn't give way.

She crunched herself, like a crawling bug, into the small space between the top of the stack of chairs and the ceiling and looked down.

A sea of grayed, bloodied faces. Yellowed eyes all wild and pleading, tongues lolling obscenely as their jaws worked, clamping down, opening, then down again in anticipation of her flesh in their mouths.

"Get away from me!"

More came.

And then some began to push and press the others, crawling over top of them. Like ants crawling over each other toward a shard of rock candy stuck halfway up the wall.

Even more poured in.

New groups pushing past and over the previous one, moving higher and higher toward her.

Her panic and terror swelled to its peak, then collapsed upon itself. Resignation. This was how she was going to die.

It didn't matter. It didn't matter anymore.

And then, she saw him.

"Oh... no."

It seemed cruel that when she'd given up, fate would deliver her yet another blow.

Her heart broke for the second time that day, as she saw the young man that had given her his heart.

But he was no longer a man.

"Oh... my Chubby man," she said, tears pouring down her cheeks.

Chubbs' skin was so gray it had turned almost white. Some of his dark makeup had smeared away, making his face all the more grim. His eyes dead, his mouth hanging open, tongue flicking against his lower lip.

"Hmmrrrunnnm!"

Just another mindless gimp now, he pressed against the others, trying to get to her flesh. To eat but not consume.

A hunger that would never be slaked.

But a hunger that drove him, drove all of them.

Karla could barely look at him but couldn't turn away. In the ugliness all around her, his was the only face she wanted to see.

Even if the man behind it was gone.

A BRAVER MAN WOULD have jumped up, spun around and faced him.

I am not a braver man.

"Hey, where are you going?"

Running as fast as I could, I tore out toward the only door in the room I could see. But before I got there, a grate flipped up from below, and three gimps crawled out.

I wasn't too worried, I can outrun zombies.

The three of them shook, trembled, twisted into creatures with fangs and claws. One of them roared at me and I stopped, and backed away slowly.

At least, the guy had a sense of humor.

Before me stood-- a lion, a tiger and a bear.

I said, "Oh, shit."

KARLA SLIPPED SLIGHTLY AND yelped, which excited the zombie mass below her even more. She pushed upward and this sent one of the chairs tumbling below.

The entire structure of plastic and metal was moving, bucking.

At any moment, it would crumble and collapse beneath her.

And she'd be a feast, torn apart by a hundred starving creatures.

Pushing up, she'd found a slight ridge in the wall. A gap-- she pushed a couple fingers through. If only I can--

Then she felt a hand at her ankle. She screamed.

Another grabbed for her and just got the edge of her t-shirt. She twisted away from it, but it held on tight.

Karla reached down and tore part of the shirt away and the zombie fell back, taking another with it.

"Jesus, I'm really going to die here," she mumbled to herself, then felt up for the ridge again.

Nothing. Just the top of a tile worn away.

Looking back over her shoulder, they were climbing higher, nearly there. She turned to at least catch sight of the face she wanted to see one last time before she died.

He wasn't there.

She scanned the faces until… yes, there.

More to the right now, farther away than closer, his Octx were clumsy in his zombie state and others could easily push past him.

Slowly, his face was getting farther and farther away.

"Oh, my baby," she said, seeing his miserable future as a broken creature, burdened by the tools that made him so powerful in life. A busted, sad toy.

"My sweet ba-- hey fucker!"

Another gimp had grabbed at her and she kicked it away, tugging her shirt from him, her olive skin exposed momentarily in the dim emergency lights.

That was when she saw something odd.

A moment ago, something had passed over… no.

She twisted around to find him again. Chubbs' face gray and dead. Tongue hanging out, licking the air.

Then, once again, she tugged at her shirt.

She saw it again.

Then, she thought she'd never feel that tug upon her face again, but indeed a very small smile crept to her lips.

INSTINCT TOLD ME TO hit the tiger first, the one in the middle.

Well, whatever instinct I might have when faced with three wild creatures.

Wild creatures. For some reason that phrase hung in my head for a moment.

"Say hello to..." I said, and pulled the trigger but nothing came out of my flamethrower. "Oh darn."

The tiger leapt toward me and I rolled away.

Back up to my feet, I tried again but the igniter had busted. The tiger rounded back, but by then I had an idea.

Pulling the trigger, I smacked the tip of the thrower onto the concrete and the spark turned into a fireball, catching the big cat midair.

Ducking, it flipped past me and landed burning.

The other cat looked toward me but was hesitant--these weren't just wild animals, they were being controlled by him, that was clear.

"Why don't you put your toy down?" He said behind me. "We could just talk."

I kept my eyes on the remaining two creatures.

"Okay, talk," I said, and looked up. One, two, three... thirteen. Above me, there were thirteen fat conduits of wires. If I could cut those or bring them down, he'd be disconnected.

I hoped.

But, my tank was low. I could either fry my two remaining or...

"No, not enough. Not enough," I whispered to myself. I didn't have enough to burn through all that conduit and wire.

So, my choice was made for me.

"Bad kitty," I said, pulled the trigger and fried the remaining jungle cat. It quickly burst into flames.

Then my flame went out.

I was out of juice.

"You must be... Hal. The one they called the General," the voice behind me said. "General of what?"

The gimp blank that had turned into a bear was winding itself in a circle, round and round, eyeballing me.

Its eyes flickered to the end of my flame thrower, unsure if I was saving fuel or...

"Or by general they mean, ha, 'basic.' General as in 'ordinary.' That sounds right," the First Patron taunted me. "Why don't you turn and face me, Mr. Ordinary?"

I let go of the flame thrower and gripped the two spikes that had been dug into my chest, pulled them out and held them up, ready if it were about to leap at me.

At least a bear, I knew.

Not that I could fight it, no. But it was an animal familiar to me.

Again, that thought stuck in my head. What was it about..?

From behind me: "Where is she?"

Briefly, my fear was that since I was Near Zombie that I'd be under its control. But, it seemed, near was not near enough to be one of the First Patron's foot soldiers.

At least I had that small piece in my favor.

Still, there was the large, snarly bear. That part wasn't going to likely go well.

"Where is she!?!"

The huge bear roared, then charged at me.

THE WRITHING MASS BELOW her was bubbling, frenzied, nearly tugging at her feet now, so close to tasting her blood and bones, the softness of her muscles, the sticky-sweetness of ripped flesh.

"Get away!" Karla yelled but this time it hadn't been uttered as some plaintive, begging remark.

As she tried to position herself just right, and she yelled again but not out of fear-- something better.

Anger.

She was ready to fight back.

Below her, blood and spittle bubbled from their mouths, which snapped at her, closer and closer each moment. Their hands pulled at the chairs just below her feet.

"Sorry, baby," she said looking down at her shirt. The image of Russell Brand stared back up. "But, I got a new fellah."

Looking up, she found his face once again.

Deep in the crowd, she found the man who had so sweetly touched her. Lost to the world, now, of the undead.

She looked back, briefly, to the mass of creatures writhing below her.

"You guys ain't ready for this," she said and spat at them. Then turned toward one corner of the room. She pulled the split part of her shirt around--

As she did, something passed over Chubbs' face... a sort of rippling.

She called to him, "My Chubby man--" then she tore her shirt a little more, from bottom to top, exposing even more skin beneath it.

From the middle of the pack of zombies, one began to shake, tremble--

"Rhnnmnnnmm!"

She tore a little more, more olive skin reflected in the light, and she said, "Come back to me."

"Ruuhmmmmrr!"

Finally, she yelled out, "Chubbs--" and split the shirt to the top, exposed herself bare-chested-- and one could say, this was man's first and best ED medicine, better than anything that could ever be put into a pill-- and she said softly: "Hammer time."

The young man began to shake, his head twisted and his body roiled, arms jetted out, came up and he spun.

The others backed away from him as he fell into full seizure, twisting and flopping on the ground.

"Come on, baby!"

He thrashed violently, his head bent backward, stretching the spin to the brink, his Octx bashing wildly, repeatedly against the floor, casting a shower of sparks.

"Come back to me," she whispered, watching, terrified by the pain ripping through his corrupted body.

Then he stopped, quiet, and the crowd of gimps, clambered back over top of him, slowly.

The mass moving in, something new for them... another meal?

From beneath them, she heard: "Hamm-MER!"

Four gimp heads, sliced from their bodies, flew up in an arc in each direction. Their four bodies fell like peels and Chubbs stood up, back on his feet.

He looked up to Karla and his eyes cleared.

"Hey baby," she said.

"Hey," he said back, still blinking away the film, and gave her what she'd wanted more than anything-- her smile.

Then, the second thing she wanted:

"Please? Uh, kill all of them."

"You got it," he said and raised his Octx, grit his teeth, and splayed out both hands, sliced down and away, another two went down in bloody heaps.

Stepping forward, crouching, he punched low, his red signs caught a couple gimps at the waist and he flipped their torsos away from their legs, which took a couple of steps before tumbling to the floor.

"Oh, points for creativity," she said as her Chubby man dispensed, faster and faster, with the crowd of attackers below her.

AS A KID, I'D had a teddy bear. Cared for it and cuddled it every night.

Only moments earlier, I'd shared that tidbit with the creature as it had swiped at me, nearly taking off my skull. But, nope. Nothing.

All those years of kindness I'd shown Mr. Brownnose and nuthin' from this guy.

Thought there was some sort of "bear code" or something. Nope. Fuck bears, then.

It leapt toward me again and I drove a spike into a shoulder. It yelped when I did, twisting its head toward me and it closed its teeth around my forearm.

It thrashed, turning and digging in its teeth.

"Arrgggh, let me... go!"

But it held tight.

With my other hand, I brought it around but under the control of the First Patron, he could see it coming and a giant paw landed on my other hand, pinning me to the ground.

It was still only the size of your average gimp, that was the material it'd be made from, but it was still terribly strong. I couldn't break free.

When it released my forearm, its blood-stained teeth then turned toward my neck.

"Nope!"

My hand came up to block it, and it chomped down hard on my fist and I heard the bones in my fingers crunch. A flash of pain washed through me.

"Ugghnn."

The pain quickly faded but my hand was useless in my defense, now.

"Where is she?"

The bear opened its jaws and came down onto my neck but stopped and didn't close them. And, then, it just lay there on top of me, its tongue pressing flat against my neck. Motionless.

"Hey," I said to it. "Usually, I prefer a couple drinks. Maybe a little dancing. Nice meal."

"Ah," I heard the voice behind me. "There she is."

Then I saw it.

The bear was dead. Its head split open by, of all things, the edge of a red, hand-held stop sign.

"Chubbs!"

"General," my friend said standing next to Karla. "Miss me?"

The remains of the bear, like the other two creatures, melted into a pool of protoplasm.

Jumping up I said, "Yeah, your girl's been all over me, man."

He laughed and she rolled her eyes.

"Hardly."

"Yes," I said. "Yes, we are."

We turned toward the First Patron, and I got my first look at him.

There was no way to discern where the man had been and where the wiring had invaded. Seated in a simple, upright examination table, it seemed the creature hadn't been strapped in, but rather secured.

Muscles had been used up, or atrophied. In a pair of tan slacks, there was only the hint of limbs. The shirt, knock-off Izod, looked like one of those big birthday balloons lost somewhere behind the couch for a month.

The sickly thin arms that draped out of the sleeves were folded together, useless.

The First Patron's head was enormous. It looked like long ropes should have been attached to it, secured, lest it float away and bump into something expensive.

I said, "The last time I saw something like that, Kathie Lee Gifford was worried a giant Underdog was going to ram into it."

The First Patron ignored me (or didn't get the pop reference) and simply said, "Karla, what's the code?"

"Clay, you know I can't--"

"There is no Clay. You and your people destroyed Clay."

"I know," she said. "Sorry about all that."

He asked again: "What's the code?" Then added, "Or I hurt your friends."

From behind us, the gate that had released the first three gimps, now another four crawled out. Then six more. Then more, I lost count.

We turned to watch as they morphed into gray wolves, big jungle cats, huge snakes, and what appeared to be a rabid squirrel.

I said, "Again with the wild animals."

Karla looked at me strangely, and I nodded to her. Something about that...

"Karla, what is the code?"

The possessed creatures moved forward, one half stalking me and the other after my man Chubbs. He lifted his Octx ready to fight if they struck.

But fighting off undead gimps is one thing.

Creatures with slashing claws and sharp teeth-- and a dozen or so at a time? More than even he could handle.

As Chubbs and I were separated from her, Karla was in the middle-- the lynchpin of our survival or the First Patron's release.

Either of those-- not both -- were about to happen.

The First Patron pushed his will through conduit above us, into the wing's independent servers and through the air around us, controlling these wild creatures as they slinked, teeth gnashing toward us.

"I think I prefer the gimps," Chubbs said.

"Yeah, I'm feelin' you, man.

She stepped forward. "Clay, listen, this gets you nowhere. Even if you got through the firewall, you don't even know what will work. That's a long way to stretch your mind."

The First Patron laughed.

"You don't know what you're talking about," he said. "The concepts I work in are beyond you. If you only understood," he laughed. "The irony! These are prototypal, evolutionary mechanisms that I've manipulated into moving me past humankind, pushed myself as a better to all of you!"

As impossible as it may seem, that actually made sense. More than made sense, it was that thing that had been echoing around the backrooms of my brain.

"My visions, so powerful now," he said, laughing again, "Weakness now becomes strength-- and as pitiful as I had been, I will be able to stretch my mind, as you say, beyond the bounds of the planet."

The animals grew fiercer as he laughed, more threatening.

"You must've gotten one rotten box of animal crackers as a kid, man," Chubbs said as a python took a lunge toward him then retreated.

The animals were getting more aggressive.

Now facing away from him, I said quietly, "The city boy was so afraid of the outdoors."

Karla's face dimmed for a moment. Then she looked to me and said, "Right."

"I'm going to ask one more time, Karla. Then I kill the fat one," the First Patron said.

"Bitch, I'm big boned."

"Who are you calling bitch?" the First Patron yelled, too thin to be frightening.

"Right," she said. "And it was a dragon that took away--" She glanced at Chubbs, a dozen snarling animals now stalking him.

Karla said to the First Patron, "You were afraid of the woods. Hated the outdoors."

"The CODE, the firewall code or they both DIE!"

She stepped closer.

"You got kicked out of the neighbor kids' game because you were scared of the monsters. The dragons on the box," she said. "You were afraid of them."

She turned and looked toward my attackers, then toward Chubbs.

Wild animals pressing in from the outdoors.

Dragons that could never be slain.

She turned back to him and said, "These are your nightmares."

"Yeah," I said. "Fear is how we survived, how we evolved-- fear of the dark, fear of death. He's turned it around. It's what gives him power."

"That means nothing to you!" the First Patron writhed in his seat, feeling so close to freedom, still not within his reach. "Give me the code! Or my nightmares become their nightmares and you'll live just long enough to witness their suffering!"

There seemed to be only one way out of here, if any. And it was right above us. I called out to Karla but couldn't say it out loud.

And, sure, as I've said my skills at conveying messages through gestures and looks, they ain't so hot. But everything was riding on this-- had to give it a shot.

Looking up, then back at her, then to Chubbs.

Then back up.

She traced my eyes, and then got a strange look on her face. A moment later--

"Last chance, Kar--"

Karla didn't wait, she bolted toward Chubbs and yelled to him, "RUN!"

Damn.

Told you. I suck at that.

Them running away? Totally wasn't going for that. Because now I've got a dozen animal nightmares bearing down on me.

And when they started running?

The animals charged.

AFTER A FEW STRIDES, Karla didn't head for the door but instead pointed to a long table along the wall. One that she'd worked from for months, while in this room.

"What do I do?"

She yelled back to Chubbs, "Quickly! Up!"

They both hopped onto the table, the animals coming right for them.

Kicking a part of the wall two or three times, she finally found the sweet spot and stainless steel shelves jutted out.

"They're retractable. We only used them when we needed them."

"Great," Chubbs said, his eyes wide, staring at the creatures closing in on them.

"Climb."

The metal shelves complained under their weight as they climbed toward the ceiling.

Climbed toward thirteen thick conduits, stuffed with wires.

The First Patron grit his teeth-- two more gimps emerged from the cellar below and twisted into huge birds, sharp beaks and talons.

"What-- whoa!"

Chubbs held up his Octx and reflected one into the wall-- it landed in a bloody splat. The other swerved and dragged a talon over his face, cutting into his cheek.

It banked in the air, kicked off the far wall and charged back.

"Why are we up here?"

Karla said, "Trust me," and then she told him what to do.

By the time the falcon was on a second approach, Chubbs steadied himself, looked toward Karla with a small grin.

"At least I get a kiss out of it," he said. Then, he took a deep breath and plunged his sharp Octx directly into two of the conduit above them. Sparks erupted, tesla bolts slipped down his body, down the shelves, spreading over the walls.

The falcon thought better of an attack, veering away at the last minute.

And he had been promised a kiss.

She looked up at her "Chubby man" as electricity coursed through him, his skin smoking slightly.

Leaning in, she kissed him on the lips-- and a connection was made-- she was enveloped by the electric field.

Three more gimps burst from out the floor.

On the other side of the room, Hal was fighting off a wild board that had him backed against the wall, its teeth gnashing into the rubber of his shoe jammed into its jaw.

"Hurry!"

Then Karla went back into her own memories, kissing the killer clown a little deeper as she did.

To the thing that frightened her the most.

Remembering the stories her father had told her.

His words echoing in her mind now like dropped glass and she, a little girl again, inched toward that room.

The dark, dark store room in the back of her father's store.

Two of the gimps on the floor had changed: one as a fox the other an alligator, they each peeled off to attack.

The third, trembled, shook and smoked.

"What are you doing?" The First Patron shouted. "Give me... what..?"

The animals on the ground pressed closer into Hal.

Hal shouted, "Hurry!"

Karla, the little girl, turned the knob on her father's store room, the light from behind her illuminating her nightmares.

That evil, evil thing!

And this room filled with them.

Hal saw the smoke and looked toward its source. One of the blank gimps had not become an animal, clawing and scratching... it was becoming something else.

The little Afghan girl wanted to cover her eyes, but no the nightmare, she needed the nightmare and she looked on at, stared at the devil's red eyes, sharp teeth, its mocking grin.

As Hal watched, a guttural roar rumbled out of the smoke and a creature began to take shape. As it did, at first...

He said, "That... impossible."

The creature flexed, bowed up and then from the smoke raised its black hands, thick legs bowed and menacing. At the top of each black boot, he saw a white ruffle of fur.

As it rose up, a red cap upon its head-- also lined with a cute fringe of white fur, at its base.

The creature growled again.

Then it said: "You've been... naughty."

The menacing swirl of black and red leapt at a nearby antelope and ripped its head off, then laughed.

And its belly, indeed shook, like a bowl full of jelly.

Hal said, "Yep. It's Santa."

Two more gimps leapt out from below, twisted into this new form. Blood-shot eyes, hands black from soot and blood, and a white frilled cap. It was the most horrible, evil looking Kris Kringle he'd ever seen but, yes, Virginia, it was a Santa Claus.

The First Patron, his data stream violated, shouted, "NO!"

Soon it was a battle between the animals of the forest and a small army of Santas, each with menacing grins, blood-shot eyes. The Santa of Karla's nightmares.

Hal saw his chance and ran for the First Patron.

But the creature still could control his creations-- the falcon swung around and, with both talons flexed, landed on Hal's shoulders, knocking him to the ground.

Pinned again, he watched as Chubbs' legs began to falter and Karla who'd used her nightmares had collapsed already in his arms.

Around the room, the Santa-on-animal violence raged but the red-suited gimps were becoming unstable, they wouldn't hold.

"Chubbs!" Hal called out. He yelled again but his friend wasn't responding.

Then, he heard the strangest thing--

From above.

From the opening in the ceiling, just outside in the hallway, a voice called out:

"Tossing Audrey Hepburn's salad!"

There was a loud crash! in the hall, then, up on two wheels, the Rascal® with Mr. Johnson at the helm righted itself with another crash! and launched across the room, the spikes tied to the front of the vehicle spearing the huge, bulbous skull of the First Patron.

Instantly, the animals shuttered, then melted into pools of protoplasm.

Chubbs had fallen away but not passed out. Holding on, he'd steadied himself and Karla, who cracked open her eyes, smiled and exhausted, and just held onto her "Chubby man."

Hal wobbled to his feet and walked over to the upended scooter.

He flipped it off and helped Mr. Johnson to his feet-- noticing that Mr. Johnson had a much stronger grip than before. Likely because his hand and arm were now larger, more muscular and more, well, black.

Still, Hal's first question was: "Do I want to even know what 'tossing salad' means?"

Johnson smiled, started to speak, stopped, then said: "No, I don't think you do." He then added: "You can google it."

"No, I don't think I'll be doing that."

WHILE CHUBBS AND KARLA talked and got some of her things, Mr. Johnson and I had made it back to the old folks home and returned. The old guy knew his way around so we were in and out quick.

And back, most importantly, with what was left of the Swordman's octogenarian's supply of ED patches. Split between us, at least three months' worth.

Chubbs, however, said he wouldn't be needing them.

"She's all the stimulation I need to keep in the NZ zone, man."

"But, of course," I said. "That means always being that way. No, you know, release. Because if you did, then, back to zombieland for you."

Chubbs frowned, looked to Karla who'd wrapped her arms around his shoulders.

"We're good with that," she said.

"We are?" he said.

She whispered to him something I couldn't hear and he smiled. Then she said, nodding to the old guy, "Is he okay?"

Mr. Johnson was near a line of trees, just this side of the truck bay. He'd asked for a moment and I'd given it to him. He'd earned it, certainly.

"Upset after losing his Rascal®," I said. "He'll be okay."

"Did you ask him about--"

"No," I said. "Not yet. Easing into it." They looked at me, stared, smiling. Hell, now I had two members of our crew that would be grinning like idiots 24/7.

And, in truth, that was fine by me.

"Johnson," I said walking up to him. He wiped his nose and spun toward me.

"General. Sorry, just..."

"Nah, don't apologize," I said. "So... how--?"

"Yeah, been waiting for ya to ask. You probably were wondering if I'd been to the 'gun show,'" he said and flexed an arm.

"No, I was wondering why you had two black arms."

He shrugged.

"The Ladies-- well, the four things we thought were them-- each took a limb and made a wish, of sorts, tore me apart. Left me for dead and as they walked away, you guys must've gotten the big-headed thing's attention, so they melted into the pink goo."

"Awful."

"But then, like how you described it, my legs and where my legs had been... they were pullin' at each other. I just scooted and schlump, they bound back together."

"The arms."

"Ah," he said, flexing again. "Well, there was a security officer nearby, dead. And my hands are a bit arthritic, so I thought, let's see if this works. And, whoo, it do!"

"You ripped off the arms of the dead guy?"

"Not just the arms, son..."

"Wha-- it? No way."

"You wanna see?"

"HELL no!" I said. "Christ, I hope you're kidding."

"You'll never know, then."

I wrapped an arm around his shoulder.

"I'm sorry about your old man scooter. I know it meant a lot to you."

"S'okay."

"You know, I was thinking we shold try to go after those trucks. The shipments contaminated with ZBF. And we've got a rig left."

"Yeah?"

"What do you think about maybe spending a day or two outfitting it before we hit the road."

"The Peterbilt®?"

"Is it? Yeah, do your Chicago outfitters thing you do."

"You got it, General."

I walked into the street and was nearly mowed down by a UPS van.

Amazing.

Chubbs and Karla came up next to me, watched as the van rounded a corner, swerved around a wandering gimp, and continued on.

I said, "The world is succumbing to a zombie virus and most of these people are just going on business as usual."

Chubbs, a man who can put things in perspective said, "Well, at least the restaurants are still open."

"Yeah," I said. "And I know a good lesbian deli nearby, if you want to grab a bite before the road."

We'll fight until every last gimp is dead, buried.

Until those who would set back the clock of mankind are extinct, themselves.

And right the wrongs of our past.

Karla, get out, this is my thing!

Whatever, Hal.

We are the ones you've heard about.

We are the turgid...

... and the flushed.

Seriously??

Go with it, Hal.

We are The Swordsmen.

Damn right.

Oh, so you'll go with that... not Swordspersons or some crap like that?

End it there, very strong, Hal.

Call me "General."

DEAR LOVELY, GOOD-LOOKING READER...

If you liked *The Swordsmen (FSGM)*, please take 20 seconds to leave a review on Amazon. This helps other readers find the novel and, no matter how short, reviews are 24k gold to an author for all those months or years of work they put into a story.

On a Kindle style reader, you can leave a review on the next page ("Before You Go"). Otherwise, click here

Thank you for hanging out with my friends.
Hey, I've got new ones!
Head over to DickWybrow.com, and I'll fill you in.

Printed in Great Britain
by Amazon

68480769R00144